True North

A Collection of Short Stories

Sterling Goodspeed

ISBN 978-1-66783-418-4

To Susan, my true believer

CONTENTS

THE TRICK

*Beginning to survey at a point delineated by a stone marker, said marker
being further located on the northwesterly corner of lands now or formerly
of Sherman, said point further marking the northeasterly corner of the
lands herein conveyed and said point being further described as being in the
westerly portion of Township Twelve Great Lot 89 of Totten and Crossfield's
Purchase, Town of Johnsburg, County of Warren, running thence ...*

It belonged to my father's grandfather. Title passed in 1894. Sixty
four acres, mostly unbuildable, save for the front field along Route 8. The
back sixty were tough, mountainside into ledge. Heavy pine growth emerging from rock. A place to get lost. And as a kid, I sure did.

It was my grandfather who finally built in the 1920s. At first it was a
three- room farmhouse heated by wood, with a dug well and no electricity.
But it evolved. Niagara Mohawk reached to the house in 1939 and a drilled
well was added in the early forties..

When my father was a young man, around age sixteen he and my
grandfather began to build what became known as " the Main House." It
was a great room off the dining room with a massive stone fireplace. The
walls were pine, cut from out back and debarked on the lot. I'm sure my
grandfather didn't know the phrase "cathedral ceiling," but he designed it
tall, just shy of eighteen feet at the roof's peak. My father said he did a lot of
the heavy lifting and although that probably should have meant something,
at the time it didn't.

1

My grandfather could work with wood but was a stone mason by trade, and clearly expected the fireplace to be his masterwork. The stone was river stone from the Hudson near Riparius, that was trucked back to the property. The fireplace was designed wide and nearly six feet deep and my grandfather was probably more concerned with the stature of his masterpiece than its heating efficiency.

Ten inches below the stone floor, he added a subfloor accessed from the back of the fireplace by a small latch laid in concrete, between two stones and flush with the base. He told my father, "We got somethin' the state don't need to see, there you go."

My grandfather did not trust the government. He resented the very concept of school tax and was certain our founding fathers never intended for a federal tax, let alone the IRS. As my father later explained, he kept his mouth shut though, didn't make waves, as they say nowadays, but he was always ready with an escape plan in the event of disaster. When my father was in his late teens, the hollow base housed firearms, along with emergency provisions like medical supplies and a limited amount of water.

Before snow fell in the early 1940s, my father, under strict direction of his father, framed in the main house and built a roof on it. This permitted Grandpa to work all winter on the fireplace and it gradually ascended, stone by stone, to the ceiling.

When Grandpa mixed the concrete to bind the stones, he showed my old man what he called, "the trick." He fetched a pail stored in the barn that was filled with garnet fragments collected over the years. As the cement mixer churned, Grandpa scooped handfuls of garnet and sporadically cast the small bits of ruby like abrasive into it. He told my father, "now just wait and see."

Two summers later, Grandpa was failing and became obsessed with completing the mantlepiece of his masterwork. He decided on maple, taken from an old tree at the edge of the back sixty before it turned to stone, gnarly pine and scrub brush. The two men cut the maple, carved the unique piece and sanded for days. Grandpa chose a darker stain than Dad had expected and then finished it with a high gloss. In the end, it made perfect sense.

The mantle was anchored to the stone with iron brackets. When completed, my father remembered Grandpa placing a level on the center of the mantle and saying, "She's plumb." A moment later he came out of his bedroom with a picture of him and my grandmother on their wedding day. He placed the framed black and white photo on the center of the mantle, paused for a moment and said, "There."

Running thence South 25 Degrees, 4 Minutes West, a distance of 1465 feet to a point of intersection with County Highway Route 8; running thence generally in a Westerly direction, as Route 8 proceeds and turns along the Northerly shoulder of said route a distance of 1800 feet more or less to a stone marker, said marker delineating the Southwesterly corner of the lands herein conveyed and the Southeasterly corner of lands now or formerly of Kilkenny, running thence...

My father's best friend was Tupper Sherman. Tupp was the only child of Mott and Althea Sherman, whose farm abutted our land just to the east. Tupp and my old man, Glen were inseparable in their youth, roaming in the deep forest near Eleventh Mountain and building a lateral extension of camps and forts well into the Siamese Pond Wilderness Area. As my father stated many times, he didn't need a playground or a new toy, he and Tupp had the woods.

Glen and Tupp were thirteen years old when the Japs bombed Pearl Harbor. They watched with envy as the local boys boarded a train in North Creek to be processed in Albany. They wanted badly to join the fight, and for a time the wilderness forts of their early years transformed into sniper's nests and airplane bombers.

Everything changed during the war. There simply were no men around between the ages of eighteen and thirty. Hauling wood, fixing cars, hunting and tasks ordinarily reserved for young men, fell to the hands of others, seventy year old men, women and thirteen year old boys.

My father explained that he and Tupp learned the concept of responsibility at an early age. They loaded supplies for old women, cut cord after cord of wood for neighbors and even began performing low level home repairs and fix it work

Each boy developed a basic understanding of electrical connections, fuse boxes, plumbing and auto mechanics. The way my old man talked, they were always busy with one project or another. He never told me much about school, but always remembered Tupp falling off old lady Shepherd's roof in the middle of a snowstorm and jump starting Roy Canton's Ford on the hill going towards town.

I asked my father what it had been like during the war and all he could answer was, "different." He once told me it was like the old times never happened. Maybe it was a distant dream that everyone had shared. For me, I think of it as a hollow time. Who would return? Who would marry, go to work? Who would we forever remember as a nineteen year old in a uniform who never came home?

Tupp and Glen got very good at what they did and during the war years became indispensable to many residents across the North Country. They argued for years afterwards about who came up with the idea of turning it into a business venture but turn it they did. At some point in 1944, T & G Enterprises evolved into a general contracting firm on Main Street in North Creek. A year or so later almost by accident, Tupp and Glen met a fuel wholesaler from Albany County. They borrowed money from my grandfather (funds most likely found in the hollow floor of the fire-place) to buy storage tanks and a single delivery truck. Thus began T & G Oil.

Christmas of 1945 was a heady season. The boys were either home or coming home. A few did not return. Business was good for two guys who had yet to see eighteen. On Christmas Eve afternoon either my father or Tupp had an idea. Whose idea it actually was depends on who you talk to, and bragging rights became a part of the joke because the idea would make them famous.

Pulling out of the yard at just after 3 p.m. with a full tank of oil on the truck, they went from Baptist to Episcopal to Catholic to Methodist to Presbyterian, topping off each churches oil tank for free. Unknown to most, they had shared a small flask of moonshine swiped by Tupp from his old man's private stash.

Tupp returned home with my father that evening. A fifteen foot tree was lit, and the tree's reflection glittered off the garnet fragments as a fire roared. Grandpa's great room as at last complete. Tupp helped my father pin fresh pine boughs over the mantle. Grandpa had slowed down but still pretended to be involved.

I haven't said my grandfather's name but it's the same as mine. Grandpa was Ellis Berton, and he knew the boys were sneaking shots of moonshine. "Aint' no harm in a taste of it Tupp, but you best not let my wife catch on."

"You wanna swig," Tupp asked.

"Pass it here before Granny comes in."

My father said Grandpa took a long drag off the bottle and walked to the warmth of the fire. He took a poker off the stand, stirred the coals and added another log. He returned the poker to the rack and turned with a smile to Glen and Tupp. "She's sure putting out some heat tonight boys." The smile faded from his face and with sudden bewilderment in his eyes he said, "what is that," before he fell face down to the floor.

Running thence in a general Northerly Direction in a fashion roughly parallel to the Eastern boundary line of the parcel herein conveyed a distance of 1464 feet to an iron marker set, said marker delineating the Northwesterly line of the subject property, running thence...

I should be telling you about my grandfather's burial. Tupp and his father Mott digging a grave in our family plot. Tupp breaking a shovel and Mott saying, "dig it right son, we only got two left." I should tell you what my father said about his mother, "vacant, in a fog, unable to grasp it, unable to mourn."

But that's not what I think of. Instead I will tell you that my father buried Ellis Berton at 10 a.m. and he and Tupp were delivering fuel by 1 p.m. He said you go on and you adjust because you don't have a choice in it.

Years later I was a teenager working for T & G Oil. My father and I were lifting empty barrels and stacking them behind the shop in North Creek. It had rained hard the day before and the land behind the shop was wet, almost boggy. We set down the barrel to take a breather and my father pointed at his muddy work boot and said, "look at this." With that he stepped forward with his right foot and pressed it firmly into the ground with all his body weight.

"Look at what," I asked, bored and edgy, the usual me circa 1969 at age eighteen.

"Not now, when I lift my foot," my father said.

With that, he raised his foot and pointed at the imprint left in the ground.

"I've seen a foot print," I said.

"Now wait on it Ellis, wait a minute."

The tread was clearly defined, about an eighth of an inch deep with some tufts of wet grass near the heel. As we watched the clarity of the tread slowly began to recede. The blades of grass struggled to lift again. A little water runoff moved in around the toe. The boot print was gradually disappearing before our eyes.

"There, you see that Ellis?"

"Do I see what?"

"It's all gone, it never happened. Nobody ever leaves a footprint. The only thing to do is keep moving."

It's probably self- serving, even condescending to say this, but it's tough being the son of a rich man in a small and poor rural town. T & G grew dramatically in the 1950s. By 1959 there were six tanker trucks and the service area had tripled. That year I was eight and my mother insisted on a Christmas photo that would be tucked inside each of the three hundred twenty- two Christmas cards my mother mailed each year. The term database hadn't been invented yet, but she had one bearing addresses and cross outs with updates and forwarding addresses. She used to say, "everything is about being organized, especially Christmas."

After several grumbled complaints, my father realized she wasn't going to give up. He contacted a photographer in Glens Falls named Dick Dean. My mother was the Methodist minister's daughter and for her this was the perfect marriage of Christian faith and family. For Glen Berton though, it was a business expansion opportunity. In the back of his mind, I'm sure he thought Dean's studio was smack in the middle of Glen Street and that he could offer highly competitive fuel pricing. When he delivered free oil to the First Methodist Church of Glens Falls on that Christmas Eve, the market seemed boundless. It was the first time Tupp hadn't joined him in the tanker.

The picture was, of course staged, but not quite. It was my mother's idea to take the shots in front of the fireplace. Dick Dean had my father place his left arm atop the glossy maple mantle that my grandfather had labored over. He was to place his right arm softly at my mother's waist. I stood in front of them, and Dean extended my mother's arm over my shoulder as if taking me under her wing.

The first five shots were awkward. I remember resting on my left foot, then shifting to the right. It was hot because mother wanted a roaring fire as backdrop. We could see Dick Dean wasn't getting the shot he wanted, so he tried to make us talk.

"Will you be going into the oil business young Ellis? Do you have a girlfriend?"

Instead of making the scene more authentic, it made things worse. Finally, my father said, "Look Dick, take two more. I'm sure Audrey will find something she likes."

I heard one click and then my father's posture shifted very slightly. Although I wasn't supposed to, I knew he had slid his hand well below my mother's waist. His timing was impeccable. As Dick Dean made a last adjustment and took the final shot, my father pinched my mother's butt, and he pinched it pretty hard.

The shutter opened. There was a clicking sound and Dick Dean stood tall, a wide grin on his mild face and shouted out, "that's the ticket."

The result was a photo of my mom, eyes wide open in surprise, her face caught somewhere between a stifled giggle and a slap. My father wore a half grin, knowing and controlled. And me? I was staring straight ahead mortified and embarrassed by what had just taken place.

Three hundred and twenty-two photos of my father secretly pinching the ass of the minister's daughter were mailed out that year. At my mother's request, a large print was framed and placed on grandpa's mantle. I have always thought of it as a picture of a picture. The photo capturing a moment in the same context and scene of its permanent location. At the center of the mantle was the photo of my grandparents and from there, so the collection grew to include my parents' wedding picture, a baby picture of me and Christmas 1959.

By 1962 T & G Oil controlled 40 percent of the Glens Falls/ Queensbury market.

Running thence Easterly, a distance of 1800 feet in a manner gener- ally parallel with County Route 8 to the point or place of beginning. Said lot containing approximately 64 acres of land, lying and being in the Town of Johnsburg, County of Warren, State of New York.

In the mid- 1970s, my father began the first substantial modifica- tion to the main house in more than three decades. He got the idea while delivering oil. Despite being business partners over an increasingly wealthy business empire, both he and Tupp made time to drive a route or two each month. It built customer base and consumer confidence. On one delivery day, Glen was invited in for a coffee and atypically, he accepted, it being his last stop of the day. The customer cut him a quick check for two hundred gallons, making the coffee even better. Looking into the large, open family room with its high vaulted ceiling, he saw something he had never seen before. There was a window in the roof. Fascinated, he stood below it and looked straight up, examining it in great detail.

"It's called a sky light," the customer said.

Within a week, dad had found a regional supplier in Albany, placed an order and began planning the installation. He had two needs: good weather and Tupp's guidance traversing the ladder with wood and glass. Unfortunately, Tupp was enjoying his newest hobby. He and a group of buddies had each purchased small planes and kept them at a local airfield.

9

They had flown off to Canada three days prior in search of the mother of all trout and Tupp would then fly to an airshow in New Jersey.

My father was working on his own, when out of nowhere Mott Sherman appeared. Mott was in his early 80s and walked with a limp, but he wasn't frail. He was grizzly, tough looking and unshaven.

"Fall on your arse trying to take that up alone Glen."

"I'm alright Mott. Got to finish it before Audrey gets back from the city."

"The hell you are. You're not as young as you once were Glen. At least let me spot you and hand the tools up."

By the 4th of July, 1975, my father, with some adept moves by Mott, had installed the first skylight in town. It had precisely the effect my father had planned. Late in the day, as the afternoon sun dropped westward, the rays touched the skylight, filtering light across the great room and reflecting it off the long ago placed garnet crystals, creating a final glittering moment at sunset.

My father and Mott shared a drink the day the job was finished. They stood beneath the skylight to admire their work.

"We did alright," Mott said.

"I'd say we did, for two old men."

"Speak for yourself arsehole."

They roared at that. Dad put his arm around Mott and a tear appeared in Mott's eye.

"Mott, what the hell?"

"I be going," Mott said.

"The hell you are, what's wrong?"

"Nothin' that can be fixed."

"Try me," said my father.

Mott stared up at the blue sky. He was a private man, unsure if he wanted to or even could share what was on his mind.

"You know Althea's had the cancer?"

"I thought she was better," my father said.

"Was…for a time. Remission, the doctor called it. But it sure come back fierce. Glen, your sky window got me out of the house, and got it off my mind for a bit anyways. I'll be going home."

Mott started for the door.

"Is there any treatment?"

"Sure there is Glen. In Boston. Four hours to drive there in an old truck. Five weeks of treatment at God knows how much."

"Christ almighty Mott, Tupp can help you."

"The hell he will. The only thing worse than charity is taking it from your own kid. That's a deal I made with myself a long time ago Glen. A man's gotta have his pride. I'll scrape the cash up someplace. Have to."

"No you won't Mott. I'll help you. I'll be paying you for the roof job. One condition. You tell no one where it comes from. Not Althea, not Tupp. No one."

A week later Mott and Althea drove out of town, south and then east to a lung cancer clinic in Boston. He was behind the wheel of a new Maverick. He had $300 in his wallet and fifty crisp $100 bills hidden in the glove compartment under the car title. When Althea pushed him to tell her how he pulled it off, he just said, "seems roofin' pays real good."

I became what I called a faux hippy. The last year of college I changed my major to geology. Geology majors had the second- best pot on campus.

11

The only better pot was in the outing clubhouse, but I couldn't go there, at least not long term.

I told my father that Nixon and Ford were the same person, that revolution was the inherent outcome of capitalism, and that oil was a fundamental right. Thus, under my mother's churching, wasn't it a sin for him to charge people for heating oil? My father was beside himself.

Bored at home and with endless energy, my mother returned to college and with her finance degree, went to work for T & G. It was a good move. In a year, she streamlined the billing system and started taking the hard first steps to diversify the company. Tupp liked to spend but she could reign him in. Tupp would say, "I'm off for a business luncheon," and my mother would quip in reply, "only PB & J's please. Or do I have to join you to mind your spending?"

My mother also worked well with the head of accounting, Melanie Densmore. Melanie had run the show for years, handling the books while Dad and Tupp plotted their next move, whether it be another town, the acquisition of a family gas company or a 50 percent share in a local lumber yard. Melanie was an accountant, but never took the board exams. She went from an entry level bookkeeper in 1970 to the head of accounting by 1980.

With Tupp and my father in their mid- 50s, the question of a successor became an unspoken issue. I half heartedly started a graduate program in geology and had a live- in girlfriend, Valerie. Valerie and I were both pot heads, but she could fake it better than me. My parents liked her, and she put on just the sort of show they wanted to see.

"I don't love Reagan but he'll pull us out of the recession."

Or "Nixon just got caught."

Or "trading with China is the future."

These words were a potent elixir to my parents. They had the effect of restoring their faith in me.

When my parents went to bed, Val and I would use a long pole to pop the latch on the skylight, lifting it high above the roof line. We stood directly below and got stoned as my parents slept down the hall. The sweet smoke lifted straight up and vented out the opening.

"You put on quite a show tonight," I said.

"It's not all show."

"It couldn't be or you wouldn't be that good at it."

She reached up and undid the top button of her blouse. Then she moved her hand down the stone fireplace as though straightening her skirt.

"You're the geologist," she said.

"Yes, your point?"

"Do you find me abrasive?"

I was high but I wasn't dead. Then there we were on the fireplace hearth as my grandparents looked on.

Being the same premises described in a deed from Lester and Anna Berton to Ellis and Lottie Berton, said deed dated August 5, 1924 and recorded in the Warren County Clerk's Office in Book 196 of Deeds at Page 200 on August 12, 1924.

Forty years after T & G began as a partnership of two teenagers too young to go to war, the business was finally incorporated. Simply, 49 percent of the shares belonged to Tupp, the other 49 percent belonged to Glen. As a token, my mother held the remaining 2 percent. I had finished a master's degree in petroleum geology, was thinking of marrying Val and was completely unemployable. I smoked much less pot and much to my chagrin found myself becoming more serious. I had become paralyzed by my own indecisiveness and by not choosing, had sealed my fate.

In late 1986 I rented an apartment in Saratoga Springs and went to work for the family business. I viewed it as a temporary outpost or maybe, as a safe place until I concluded my doctorate or the opportunity I could not identify presented itself.

At first, I wasn't good at my job. I managed 400 accounts and reported to Melanie Densmore and my mother. Val landed a gig with a small investment firm in Albany. Late at night, usually on a Sunday, I would tell myself, "there, now you've settled in the precise life you were determined to avoid."

However, to my surprise, something strange happened after a year and half. While going about my business and quietly surviving, I began talking extensively to my mother. Mom was not only a worrier but also a chronic, highly organized worrier. She cited the Arab oil embargo of 1973 as first awakening. This was soon followed by the late 70's recession, the hostage crisis, national debt and the health care crisis. For her, the greatest threat to the family business was, oddly enough, oil. She proclaimed one day, over a container of cottage cheese, "the company will perish Ellis; it will surely perish if we don't diversity ourselves."

In an odd way, it was the complexity of my mother's fears that actually started me thinking creatively about the company. If I did small things, no one really noticed or cared. I began to move a percentage of profits to Val's investment company and strategically invested in alternative energy in addition to oil start ups in New Orleans and Alaska. We did well enough in a rough market to keep doing it. Melanie Densmore suggested increasing the percentage of draw moved to the investment portfolio.

Jeremy Wilson, a former fellow grad student, traveled extensively after graduation in lieu of going to work. We had once talked about traveling to Antarctica together post grad for field work analyzing what scientists were calling climate change. But the trip had never panned out. While visiting Val and me in 1989, he used a word I had never heard before: internet.

He was working in Silicon Valley for a software startup and convinced us to invest. I moved 4 percentr of the company investment account the next Monday into a company run by Larry Ellison. The company was called Oracle. I drafted a corporate resolution which my father and Tupp signed, loaning me $50,000.00 for a down payment on a house. Instead, I dumped the money in Oracle. Tupp and my mother understood the actual nature of the investment. My father was left in the dark and truly thought he was buying us a house.

Tupp had flown off to fishing camp in Canada. My father was on a self- imposed fuel run in Lake Luzerne and my mother was analyzing new fuel oil accounts. They hadn't changed but the company had.

All seemed right in my world until my mother phoned me that afternoon to tell me Melanie Densmore and my father had been skimming 10 percent of gross proceeds off the books for more than a decade while apparently fucking each other senseless on a boat they shared on Lake George. To make things worse, Tupp had phoned Mom and said, "six and a half days and not even a bite."

I never knew until then that my mother was part gangster.

From her desk she drafted a corporate resolution firing the entire accounting staff except for herself and me. Intent on fully de-balling my old man, she drafted a second resolution authorizing 100 shares of unissued stock to be sold to her, ultimately giving her and Tupp control of the company for the foreseeable future. Finally, a third resolution severed the investment arm of the company from fuel sales to establish a second authority for its management by Ellis Berton.

She then drove her Ford Explorer to the local Shell station, filled it up and headed off to Canada to secure Tupp's signature. She had brought the secret back up ledger found in Melanie's locked desk, along with a picture of Glen and Melanie in a restaurant in Bolton Landing.

Tupp took it real hard. At first, he tried to kick her out. When she presented the photo, it gave him pause. After an hour with the ledger, he knew she was right. His best friend had stolen from him for more than a decade. Their relationship had been a sham. Tupp became depressive, wouldn't speak. Instead of anger he was overcome with a feeling of loss and ultimately shame.

Tupp pulled two Molson Bradors from the camp fridge, opened them and handed one to Audrey.

"Where do I sign," he said.

Further being the same premises conveyed in a deed from by Lottie Berton individually and as executrix of the Last Will & Testament of Ellis Berton to Glen Berton and Audrey Berton, as Tenants by the Entirety, said deed dated November 14, 1946 and recorded in the Warren County Clerk's Office in Book 463 of Deeds at Page 363 on November 21, 1946.

My father and Tupp had always retained the local North Creek bank for primary banking services, including payroll, operations and a real estate investment account. All told, there was nearly $800,00.00 in liquidity in T & G Oil. As head of accounting, Melanie Densmore had authority, without limitation, to move funds from account to account, to cover payroll, pay estimated taxes and as my mother correctly surmised, moving small amounts of cash to an account with Glen. Audrey couldn't do anything about the joint account, but she damn well could protect the other assets.

With just three bars of cell service as she headed south from Tupp's secluded cabin, Audrey called the bank. The teller who took the call said branch manager Jeannine Porter was tied up on a conference call with other branch managers. My mother said simply, interrupt her, I'll wait."

A moment later, she was connected to Jeannine Porter. She advised the branch manager to cancel all access to T & G accounts by anyone other than herself or Tupp. When questioned, she explained that she and Tupp were majority stockholders, and the resolutions confirming this would be personally delivered in three hours. She further warned that if her instructions were not followed explicitly, all accounts would be closed and transferred to a competing bank in Glens Falls.

About an hour later, Melanie was denied electronic access to the company accounts. While searching her desk, she discovered the private ledger and other financial documents were missing. She knew the writing was on the wall. Retrieving only her purse and car keys, she stepped away from her desk and arrived at the bank, driving the Audi purchased for her by Glen. A short time later via bank draft she drained $60,000, the total balance of the secret bank account shared with my father. Jeannine Porter stood watchfully a few feet away from a nervous teller.

Unbeknownst to anyone, Tupp had taxied out of the small grassy Canadian airfield immediately after my mother had left for home. He was planning on beating my mother back to the shop. I suppose he thought it was still fixable, particularly if it were just him and Glen in a room. He knew though that it was the whole thing that had to be made right, not just the money.

In one afternoon, my father lost his wife, his mistress, his best friend and his business. Tupp approached him in the truck bay between two tankers.

"Can we talk before we fight," Tupp asked.

With that my father threw a wild punch, decking Tupp on the concrete floor near a metal drain. He paused and stood over him for a moment, as if in disbelief that he had actually done it.

My father had arrived at work in his refurbished 1957 Dodge and left the office in the same truck. He bought a six pack at a convenience store and arrived home around 5 p.m. We found a shot glass on the maple mantle, and I believe he considered doing it there but thought better of it.

17

Tupp found him on the back sixty. One bullet in his mouth and a photo labeled Christmas 1959 next to his body. There were no calling hours. It was too raw to gather.

Oracle stock, of course, went through the roof. Val never returned to the investment firm after her maternity leave. That Christmas Eve, Tupp showed up at the main house on Route 8 with the oldest tanker still in operation. He loaded my mother, partially by force into the front seat, and drove to the churches, topping off each tank. They drove back to the house in silence. Mom thanked him, shook his hand and invited him in.

As Val and I watched, my mother cleaned soot and ash from the fireplace and used a crow bar to access the hidden compartment.

"It has to be here Tupp. There's no other place he could have put it. You and I both know there is still money missing."

I went over to finish what my mother had begun. I fitted the bar into the small latch and carefully lifted the door. Tupp shined a flashlight into the back of the fireplace and sure enough, there it was. Over a million dollars, in cash, skimmed off the corporate books all those years.

My mother counted it and put just over $600,000 into a duffle bag for Tupp. It was awkward but it was over with.

"I'll walk you out Tupp," my mother said, tears welling in both eyes.

"I'm sorry it had to happen like this," Tupp said, as he and my mother reached out and clasped hands.

"I suppose we knew there'd never be a happy ending," Tupp said.

The weight of the duffle bag seemed too much for him as they made their way towards the door. It was odd to think it, but if my mother hadn't held his hand to mark the balance point, he might well have been dragged to the floor by the cash. Together they seemed so weary and beaten down.

A moment later, as Tupp said his goodbyes, a distant figure appeared, crossing the property through drifted snow. It was his father, Mott Sherman. Mott was ninety now and rarely went outside.

"You two stay there," Mott said.

"Pa, what are doing, you'll catch pneumonia."

"Stick right there," Mott said.

"I'm here."

"Where's young Ellis?"

"I'm here Mott," I said.

Mott spoke. "I need to break a promise tonight. I need to tell Ellis something I gave my word never to speak of. Years ago, your Pa opened the fireplace for me. He gave me money to take Althea to Boston, bought me the Ford I'm still driving. He wasn't all bad young Ellis. You see, he stole from his partner but used some of the money to save his partner's mother." He continued, "turns out he was a lot like all of us. He was a mixed bag."

Further being the same property conveyed by Audrey Berton as surviving tenant by the entirety of Glen Berton to Ellis Berton and Valerie Berton, husband and wife, said deed being recorded in Book 953 of Deeds at Page 91 on September 5, 1991.

I became the CEO of TG Adirondack. By the time I was in my mid 40s the company had become a multi headed beast. Oil and delivery remained a cornerstone, as did the investment wing. In the mid 1990s we were able to secure a majority interest in our wholesaler and became involved in distribution in several states. Tupp spent most of his time in Canada and had formally resigned from active participation in the corporation.

Mom protested fiercely when I moved to purchase a 20,000 square foot office complex in Saratoga, but still cut the ribbon at opening. She and her sixteen- year old grandson Dylan, hung a picture on the lobby wall of

Dad and Tupp with that first tanker back in the 1950s. We were rich but sometimes felt like we didn't have anything. Mother spent six months of the year on Sanibel Island, Florida and the other six months in Glens Falls. We rarely spoke of my father and when we did, it was guarded. I sometimes wondered, what would you do if you could do anything? What would you have if you could have anything? How would you behave if you didn't have to? We made more money annually than our accountants projected. Valerie was a key part of it. She had serious street cred when it came to analyzing emerging energy companies. Dylan was starting to look at colleges and I was quickly approaching the age where my old man had taken his life.

In the Spring of 2010 my mom arrived from Florida with a surprise announcement. She would not be staying that summer in Glens Falls. She had decided to reopen the main house in Johnsburg. Over everyone's objections, she opened the house in June. She was in her mid- eighties then, and had no business relocating to the middle of nowhere, but she couldn't be stopped.

The house had been closed for more than a decade. She refused to hire help and set about cleaning every inch of it herself. It surprised me when she cleaned and returned the family pictures to their precise place on the mantle of the great fireplace. It seemed like a physically symbolic effort to return order to what had been torn apart.

Dylan was a recently licensed driver, and he gladly accepted my request to go up and check on grandma. Most times she fed him and sent him back south with various assurances of her well being. He often brought college catalogues and asked her to help him decide. It was a role she thoroughly enjoyed.

Mother invited all of us for dinner on the 4th of July. Val was in the kitchen as I came inside. Dylan and my mother were in front of the fireplace and I paused to hear their conversation. She pointed at the old pictures.

"Don't ever let anyone tell you your grandfather was a bad man. He was the best man there ever was."

She talked more openly with Dylan than she ever had with me.

"He built everything we have. He's responsible for all of it. And I..." she trailed off.

We watched the fireworks in North Creek that night, something we hadn't done in decades. For the first time in years, I saw a glimmer in my mother's eyes during the finale.

"I always want to remember this", she said.

That night we decided to stay at the main house instead of driving south. My mother poured herself a rare glass of wine. After Val turned in and Dylan was in another room, she told me we needed to talk.

"I'm sick," she said.

"How sick," I asked.

"We're all going to get sick Ellis, it's in the cards for all of us. It seems I have cancer."

"That's why we're in Johnsburg, isn't it," I asked.

"That and another thing," she said.

"What other thing?"

And then she told me about Tupp.

"You see my sweet Ellis, I loved them both, and in the end, nearly destroyed all three of us.."

Subject to the right of Mott Sherman, his heirs, successors and assigns, to cross the rear portion of the subject premises for the purpose of drawing water from time to time from the Mill Creek.

Valerie found us at 3 a.m. My mother had poured another glass of wine and I had made camp in my old man's recliner with an afghan wrapped around the lower part of my body. Val woke me and working together, we got my mother to bed. Remarkably, the second glass of wine had remained fixed and un-spilled in her left hand as she fell asleep, having never taken a drink. We waited for her while she was in the bathroom. Valerie found the oral chemo and got her water to wash it down.

She was back asleep as soon as we put her in the bed. I'm not sure she was ever fully awake. I brought my mother's wine to bed with me. I sat on the edge of the bed finishing it while Val laid next to me, her head propped on her elbow.

"Well, what was that," she asked.

"I guess you'd call it the big talk," I said.

"Did you find out why she came back here," Val asked.

"Oh yes."

"Well?"

"To show loyalty to my father," I explained.

"Why was she so compelled to show loyalty when he was the one who was unfaithful?

"Because..." I trailed off.

"Because why?" Val demanded.

"Because it turns out to be a lot more complicated than that."

"I mean you no disrespect, but your father had a decades long affair under your mother's nose and stole company money for most of that time," Val said.

"All true but..."

"But what," Val again demanded.

"She feels she drove him to it."

"Did she?"

"I really don't know."

"I didn't even know she was sick until I saw the prescription," Val said.

"She told me that first."

"Is it bad?"

"Long term, it's terminal. She probably has a few months."

"Is she handling it?"

"A lot better than I am. She's reconciled to it. It turns out the diagnosis forced her to reconcile with the rest of it," I said.

"So tell me."

"I promise I will tomorrow when we have a few minutes. None of this to Dylan yet, ok?"

Valerie rolled over and sighed.

"I certainly can't tell him what I don't know," she said.

I finished the wine and laid down.

"In the morning, I promise. I'm not sure I have it figured out enough to explain it to you."

Also subject to any other easement, right of way or license of record encumbering the subject premises.

"In many ways I'm sure you remember your father as a bull. He was a motor, going every waking hour," my mother told me.

"That he was," I said.

"But there was something else to him you didn't know. The only people who knew it were Tupp and I."

"Ok."

"You know how they argued about who bought the old tanker?"

"Of course, that's part of the fable isn't it?"

"It seems so but it isn't really. Your father bought the tanker with money from your grandfather," my mother explained.

"Is that important?"

"It is. He had a gut instinct about the risk. He brought Tupp along. Tupp even confirmed it to me."

"Ok."

"Driving to the churches."

"Yes, every Christmas Eve."

"It was never Tupp's idea. He claimed it but it was your Dad. The same with marketing in Glens Falls and Saratoga."

"I had no idea," I said.

"He took Tupp along with him and in some ways, he took me too."

She pulled herself from the chair and went to the kitchen. She poured a second wine, unheard of for her. I felt a chill and reached for an afghan nearby.

"You knew the bull, the worker, but he had this other thing and you might as well know, you have it too. He could miss 90 percent of what was going on around him and then make a decision that in retrospect was life altering. You found out about Oracle but you didn't have to buy in. I bet you've never looked back on the valuation but the gain on your initial investment totals 480 percent. The gain on the company stock fund during your time managing it was 26 percent annually. You couldn't explore energy markets. but you knew Val could and let her run. It's a gift," she said, now getting tired.

24

"I think I've been lucky," I said. "I think you're right though, looking back and hearing it from you, I think he had something more."

"He was the most intuitive person I have ever known, but not always. He might be figuring out a way to buy the highway, but in the process get hit by a bus."

We both laughed.

"So he took Tupp and I along. And Tupp and I became dear, dear friends."

"Friends?"

"When your father built the skylight with Mott, I was in New York City. The company paid for me to go to a conference there. I can't even remember what it was about. Computers, I think. And Tupp went to an airshow in New Jersey. He took me to dinner. Dear God, we laughed and laughed."

"You don't have to do this Mom."

"That dinner was the last time I had a second glass of wine Ellis, until tonight."

She paused for a moment and explained that it was easy for her to get tired now.

"Then why don't we get to bed," I suggested.

"I've come this far. All Tupp could talk about that night was about when they were just starting out. Shoveling roofs, fixing cars and mending circuit breakers during the war. He remembered your father bringing me to the first shop on Main Street in North Creek in lieu of a real date. And this one too I had forgotten. How he strapped you in the front seat of the tanker when you were eight months old and took you on your first run."

She paused again, catching her breath. She briefly stared at the mantle with the returned old photos.

"Tupp never married. He told me there wasn't room for it. I put my hand on the table. Fifth Avenue seemed a long way from a fuel company in the Adirondacks. He put his hand on top of mine. I cried for no reason, and he shook his head. I loved him for what we had in common, our history, the business, your father. We didn't even talk of it. That is all. We smiled at each other and said we loved each other without saying it."

"And that's it," I asked "That's the whole thing?"

"No, not quite. You see your father sensed it, sniffed it out like a new venture. He knew about the bond, about Tupp and me. It was his gift gone bad. There was no affair Ellis. I was never unfaithful as it is defined. But your father knew I loved Tupp too and it ate away at his insides. It drove him mad."

"But nothing happened."

"You see though, it did in a way and he sensed it. It drove him to Melanie and everything that followed was a consequence of his insight into something that didn't occur but could have."

The next morning Dylan cooked us bacon as a treat. My mother smiled at me with a sense of relief that she had cleared herself of it. Later I explained it all to Val. The three of us drove south and left my mother there alone, where she wanted to be, an odd final statement of loyalty to my old man. I looked back and saw her stoically on the porch wearing what she always called a "house dress" and for a moment I had the oddest of feelings. I wondered to myself, which one was she remembering while standing on the family porch. 'Entangled' is the word that wouldn't leave my mind as we headed south. I smiled about my father taking me out in the tanker when I was eight months old and felt a softness for old Tupp, someplace in a fishing camp in Ontario, soon to be the last one left in a triangle that really didn't have sides.

26

Now being the same premises conveyed by Valerie and Ellis Berton to Dylan Berton by deed being electronically recorded in Book 1572 of Deeds at Page 462, reserving a life interest to the use and enjoyment to the premises to the parties of the first part.

SKIING TO SCHOOL

Listen, I think I may finally be as old as I feel. Mother freshly buried in the Catholic cemetery in North Creek and me with years into retirement. Someone asked me, "did you inherit?" But with everybody gone I almost said, "only responsibility." Not for just their belongings, I might add, but finally mine too.

Many years before, winter had been Claire's favorite season. She remembers it now as a time for tobogganing by moonlight and skiing to school. From where she sits, she sees her little girl figure bundled tightly against the cold, tramping up the back slopes to the top of the mountain behind her house. She aches to catch her brother's stride so as not to be left behind. Secretly, however, she knows the game he plays, staying far enough ahead to motivate her fear of losing him, but close enough to listen for the regularity of her strides.

Back fifty years ago, distance meant something. The caretakers' house near the garnet mine founded by Henry Hudson Barton was twelve miles by road from the Village of North Creek. The first five miles paralleled the west side of the Hudson River. The last seven turned directly off the state road and gradually climbed the back of Gore Mountain. The house was one hundred yards below its summit, and from the top of Gore, North Creek was two miles straight down. As good as it was, their father's truck was rendered useless by a major storm, and on those days, they struggled through the drifts and ascended the mountain's rear side.

If winter was Claire's favorite season, November was a month of longing. Longing for the scent of evergreen and the sound of rustling Christmas paper. But longing most of all for a great Nor'easter that would leave her family snowbound in the tiny mountaintop mining village, abandoned but for the guest house where her father and mother served as caretakers. On those days, their father's truck would go no further than the end of the driveway. Inevitably, he would slam the driver's door in disgust and turning to her brother Gerald, utter the magic words they longed to hear, "only way you're gettin' down this mountain today is on skis."

Here is a book of children's verse, rhymes remembered in mother's soothing bedtime voice, and here is Gerald's report card from before the war. These are the photos of Gerald's high school graduation and the varsity letter he earned as starting forward on the basketball team. Here's a picture of little Tommy Barrett, their childhood companion. Here is her ancient charm bracelet, it jingles as she lifts it, the tiny stars and heart dancing to life. The stars were a gift from mother for Christmas in 1935 and the heart, a gift from Tommy a year and two days before they were married. Here's Tommy in uniform, and one of Tommy and Gerald together in the Philippines. In smudged pencil the photo's reverse side reads, "Solomon Islands, 1943."

Breathing hard, legs already burning from the climb, Claire is last to reach the top of the mountain. When she arrives, her brother and Tommy have already fastened the raw hide straps around each heel of their work boots and are making last minute adjustments to their mittens and caps prior to descending. Though Gerald will tease her about being as slow as an old woman and left behind to freeze on the mountain, she knows that he has waited deliberately and will give her a solid head start before he pushes off from the top.

She has begun the sorting. Here is father's obituary, a yellow paper tearing slightly as she unfolds it. Dated January 15, 1965, it states that her father William Preston, had for many years served as caretaker for the huge guest house in the mining village and had also been a mountain guide for downstate hunters. It tells how in the 1930s, he was a chauffeur at the Olympic games in Lake Placid and had picked up French from transporting European skiers to and from their events. He had been retired. He had died after a lengthy illness. He had been survived by his wife May and a daughter Claire. There had also been a son.

Cold has made the evergreens atop the mountain brittle. A strong wind in the night can break their tips off. Many will grow in perfect form for thirty or forty feet and then stop suddenly where the upper portions of the trunks have been torn away. As she fastens her bindings (mittens off and racing to finish before the cold steals her coordination), she thinks that the trees exposed on this barren and rocky slope contrast sharply with the world her parents have created on the backside of the mountain.

Her house, with its giant stone fireplace, ablaze last night after dinner, must be the warmest place in the world. Her father, long before snow fell, cut enough wood for winter. How many nights did she sit spellbound before the dancing yellow and blue flames and fall asleep in the overstuffed chair until mother carried her off to bed?

At last, she straightens herself, and lifting her leg, shakes her foot from left to right as Gerald has taught her to do. This makes sure the binding is fully secure before she makes her first turn.

The wind is blowing softly, but cold. She pushes to the edge of the hill, inches away from the balance point, which once passed, will allow her form to be pulled towards earth like a falling star.

Looking back, she sees her brother nod. The signal. She pushes and is gone.

Here is the *handwritten letter dated October 7, 1944:*

Mr. & Mrs. Preston,

It is with deep regret that I inform you of your son Gerald's death in the line of duty. Your son was a brave boy and a good soldier. He was liked by all the other boys over here and never did anything to dishonor himself or his family name. He spoke of you often and about getting home to the mountains to make a living. He died almost instantly when he was struck by a Japanese mortar fragment. Again, I am awful sorry.

Sincerely,
Staff Sgt.
Edward S. Martin

Claire cannot see them but knows intuitively they are skiing behind her. Tommy tucked low and turned little, gaining as much speed as possible. Gerald, making his long, sweeping turns, in full control at every moment.

They are skiing an ancient logging trail and as they descend the mountain terrain, the evergreens are replaced intermittently by stands of birch and maple. The snow is very deep. It is difficult to turn. She knows that she will have to turn less and ski faster if she is to avoid walking on the flatter portion of the mountain.

Turning a bend in the trail, the path suddenly widens, and they glimpse the rising chimney smoke from the woodstoves of the village far below. It is so cold that the white smoke rises in straight funnels, high into the winter sky. The clouds too, are made of smoke. It's as if an invisible force from heaven is pulling air from earth to fill the sky.

Her legs are taut, and her elastic lungs are sucking in the frigid air. She forces herself to turn less and speed up to avoid walking the flats. She knows her brother will need to decide whether to risk skiing at her pace or

31

tuck into a ball and coast into town. Fleetingly, she remembers the warmth emanating from the stone fireplace.

Tommy is well ahead and will not need to walk. She senses Gerald is ever closer behind her. She knows he is not turning. His decision has been made. He will pass her and coast to town. This is the furthest up the mountain he has ever allowed himself to pull ahead of her. With the mining village far behind them, it is as if they are skiing to another world. A world of algebraic equations, Knights of the Roundtable and the best five on five basketball ever played in the high school gym, where the town team still plays on Friday nights.

Here are the wedding pictures, and then pictures of Claire's children, Angela and Steve, riding a pony at the county fair. Their father steadies the horse and holds a hand on their legs to help them feel secure. Now it is Angela and Grandma May (she looks so frail) standing in front of a Buick Skylark, Angela's first car. Here we are celebrating Mother's 70th birthday, gathered around a giant cake which proclaims, "Happy Birthday with all Our Love, Claire, Tommy, Angie and Steve."

Suddenly her throat is parched, and she feels a tightening in her chest. She knows well what the paper says before she unfolds it. There is a picture of Thomas D. Barrett, along with his age, 59. The story tells what she knows firsthand. Tom died unexpectedly. That Friday is engraved in her memory. He came home early from work, poured himself a cup of coffee and relaxed in his recliner in front of the tv, as he had so many times. She heard Jim Rockford's voice as she puttered in the kitchen, a show Tom had watched many times. She found him there during a commercial, his face blue, his coffee cold, the TV Guide open on his lap. She dialed 911 and asked for an ambulance.

Claire is completely out of control when she reaches the flats. Worse, her thighs ache, and as she tries to steady herself, her legs shake beneath her. Gerald is far beyond her now, nearly to the edge of town, and even if she screamed, he is too far away to hear.

The depth of the snow makes turning difficult. She is too tired to carve her turns as Gerald has taught her. She senses her weight shifting from left to right and moves to compensate. She concentrates on turning as tightly as possible, shifting her weight to her downhill ski and trying to slow down. As she turns, there is a tightness in her left foot as it cramps up. The cord of muscle between her toes and heel has locked itself in a spasm of pain and she cannot complete the turn.

She suddenly has a sense of being underwater alone. Swimming in this half- conscious state, she is aware of Gerald and Tommy's existence amidst whirlwind of forest and houses. Then, there is nothing but snow. Her body is turning about. She is outside of herself, a spectator of her own circumstance. Gerald will call her an old woman. Father will never allow her to ski again.

Something's not right with her leg. It dangles as she spins across the surface of the snow. She has heard evergreens being snapped apart by the night winds. Instinctively she knows, she knows her leg is broken. Finally, she comes to rest in the powdery white. She almost laughs at the thought of making a snow angel without limbs.

As she stops, the excruciating pain begins. Her leg is on fire. When she breaths, she tastes blood in the back of her throat. She tries to move and cries out in pain. Her britches are soaked with urine. She's never fallen badly and is now below the snow, crying for her brother, Tommy or her mother or father. She will die here, she thinks, and her frozen corpse not found until Spring. For the first time she is alone.

Funerals bring us back to clean the houses of our childhood. The treasures of yesteryear, the last memorials to a life lost, become the survivors' responsibility. Realities of November 22 1984, Mother's funeral subside with each rediscovery. These are the memories of her childhood, perhaps the only things she truly owns. She will do with them as she pleases.

The pain Claire feels as she walks the empty house of her youth is of an exquisite sort. To be torn so deeply by a death must be an indication of the success of her life. Mother's funeral is over. She must clean this house herself if she wants it complete.

Standing at the window she looks across the back slope that leads up the mountain. A brutal wind spins the snow about. She shivers, but knows the house is not cold. She could cry, she thinks, but who would hear her? She recalls the morning nearly fifty years ago when she skied to school and fractured her leg.

She builds a fire in the old stone fireplace, aware that the chimney hasn't been cleaned in many years. The darting flames seduce her and even the illusion of cold is gone. Sunk deeply in the overstuffed chair, she is awake but drowsy. To her surprise, she feels a sense of satisfaction at having accomplished so much in only a day's time. Her possessions packed neatly in cardboard boxes and bound tightly with yarn from Mother's knitting basket makes her feel like a child with a collection of stamps or clippings to present at school.

Somewhere distant in the house, a wind gust causes a storm window to rattle softly in its casing. For a moment she is startled, but then remembers.

ARTIFACTS

I'm Jack Drum and it's another normal Saturday night in Smalltown, USA. This is the place you see on the postcards, ancient wooded mountains, glistening trout streams, kids frolicking along the shoreline of a pristine Adirondack lake while Mom and Dad smile glowingly between the pitched tents and barbeque. Don't believe a fuckin' word of it.

Here's my postcard. Former wife's sister is squatting to pee by the old rail line. Amanda Stake. She's divorced like me so it's not like "immoral." She kept her married name Stake, but sometimes uses her maiden name in the middle. Amanda Majestic Stake is pretty hammered and pretty close to tipping over as she wipes herself. Behind her I know is the Hudson River, encased tonight (this morning) in fog, not visible but as much a certain presence as a surgical scar. She stands up, retrieves her cigarette and looks into the fog. What can she see? Nothing. Barely even make out the old steel on the nearby rail bridge. She's still smoking. I've got a pint of JD in between my legs but I won't need much after the last four hours.

I can see her walking back towards me now, stamping out the cigarette, reaching for the truck door. It's a relationship of convenience as much as anything. Same town, same enemies. Saturday night, get drunk, cry a little. Maybe she lets me feel her up a little. She feels a lot like Marlene. If I'm drunk enough, it's confusing. And if I'm lucky enough, she'll give in to a hand job. I know it's her way of getting me off her back and for me it's not like the real thing. It's having someone else do something you could do yourself. It's pretend sex, make believe connection. But ever since her sister decided she was sleeping with Jesus and couldn't cheat on the lord with me, a hand job from her unsaved sibling amid a solid beer buzz and the truck filled smell of menthol cigarettes has to be enough.

She's getting up into the truck. She smiles. She says, "let's smoke a joint first and I'll make you feel good."

"Sounds alright," I say.

A minute later she runs her hand down the inside of my leg and faces me with her eyes closed and the lit joint in her mouth. She takes a deep hit, rolls her eyes open and hums softly as she moves her hand.

* * *

It might have been better if the mine had just closed overnight. You know, like ripping a band aid off your arm. Get it over with quick. But that's not what the big boys in Dallas had in mind. Closed it incrementally over several years. nineteen men laid off. Twenty-Six men laid off. Another fifteen men laid off. It reminded me of when Cronkite would list the number of dead men killed in Vietnam a few years earlier. Seventeen men today in Southeast Asia. Twenty Five men. Tet. Titanium. Same difference.

There was no local economy to absorb us. The money hurt quick, but a good number of us got done in by the loss of hospitalization. No coverage for wife or kids. A kid's broke leg could be fatal to a family. If you had worked anywhere near the chemical lab you knew you'd need coverage sooner or later.

I lasted longer than most. I managed the furnace. They took front end laborers, eventually my crew. One of the managers liked me. He moved me to security. It was a 20 percent pay cut but it bought a few months.

So when it happened, strange enough, it still felt like a surprise. I stopped for a six pack at Murdie's Store in Minerva and didn't think of mentioning it. I drove into North Creek with a cold Bud in the cup holder and turned left in Wevertown onto Route 8 towards home. This is where Garrow took the campers. There was a lumber company there. I almost stopped to inquire about work but thought better of it with beer on my breath.

I told Marlene straight up. Finished a third beer.

"God help us," she said.

"God ain't going to cut us a paycheck," I said.

"And you didn't need to drink part of the last one either Jack."

* * *

When you get poor, it takes up most of your time. We heated with wood, so that was something. We owned part of a small woodlot in Thurman and I took two full cords off it before I had to sell my stake for cash. For awhile I had a full woodshed, an unemployment check every couple of weeks and $2000 cash from the land sale.

Hindsight's twenty-twenty. I shouldn't have been dippin' into the cash to fund Friday nights at Basil's but I was bored out of my mind. There was no hope for regular work. Lumber company, not hiring. Local contractor, try another time Jack. We got no work.

Prescott Jackson was a touring preacher with a Pentecostal church centered in Seattle. Why he ended up preaching at a church in Glens Falls in the summer of 1979 is beyond me. She started disappearing for days at a time, said she was part of a mission. She started to dress differently, carried a bible in a soft green leather case. One morning that August she looked back at me as she went out the door and with a note of solemn, devout disgust, said, "I'll pray for you."

I've never heard of a QDRDO but sure enough Marlene took 50 percent of my future retirement, not that there was much to start with. I'm sure Preacher Jackson paid for her lawyer. I called around but everyone wanted a grand down.

So I started a drinking game at Basil's that summer. The game was called "Pro Se." When the juke box was between songs or there was a brief, quiet lull, I'd stand on my bar stool and shout, "Pro Se." That was the signal for everyone to drink.

That summer, every time a kid came in and played the jukebox, it was that Goddamn song, "My Sharona," over and over again.. It drove me nuts. I like Merle Haggard, Johnny Cash, even old Elvis songs, but Sharona played the whole fuckin' summer.

One Saturday, at 2 a.m., parked at the bar with a boiler maker to end the night, a good memory. It's quiet and we're at last call. Someone put fifty cents in the jukebox and I remember saying to myself, "if it's the fuckin' Knack I'm going to off myself."

It took me a minute to recognize the first guitar notes and the deep voice. The kids were still home from college but someone had stolen the music and played "Jackson," by Johnny and June Carter Cash.

"By God, I've been saved," I said out loud.

I leaned into the bar and with great effort stood straight up and shouted to anyone who would listen, "Pro Se."

On cue, everyone drank. A minute later Amanda Majestic appeared by my side with a martini in one hand and a cigarette in the other.

"How about you buy me a drink partner," she asked.

* * *

I find a man does what he has to to get by. I knocked around in the early 1980s with a logging crew. It was all under the table which was alright by me. I never understood what FICA was even when I was making real money at the mines.

It was a long trip back but I finally got on at the mountain blowing snow. It wasn't year round but it was steady, November to March. Better than I'd had in a long time. There was my old friend FICA again. I felt the pace come back into my life and I liked it.

I think everybody talks to themselves in one way or another. Late that Spring I said to myself, "you don't never do anything for the joy of it." That thought was in my brain for a couple of weeks until very much out of character, I did something rash.

It was eight years old but it ran good and it was a Harley. The next Friday I did something even more rash. I phoned Amanda Majestic and told her I'd like to pick her up early.

"I got nothing else going on," she said.

"Good, I'll pick you up at 4 p.m." And wear long pants."

Two hours later, Amanda laughed and squealed as I turned the bike off State Route 28N onto Blue Ridge Road. From there, a quick left onto Tahawus Mine Road.

"You ever been up here before," I asked.

"I never been."

"Drove this road to work twenty- two years. Not a place like it I ever seen."

I stopped the bike near an impressive stone structure.

"It's kind of creepy," she said. "Like somebody's going to walk out of one of those old houses."

I pointed to the massive stone.

"That's McIntyre Blast Furnace, or what's left of it. Part of the old iron mill."

"How old is it."

"Early 1800s. Nice place to ride to, isn't it?"

"Yeah it is."

"And that one, that's famous, that's the McNaughton House. Teddy Roosevelt slept right in there."

"When did it all die?"

"That's a harder question than you might think. It actually died twice. So, it's a ghost of a ghost town."

I reached into the saddle bag and pulled out two cold beers.

"In the 1850s she went belly up for the first time. Problems with the ore and the fact that they were in the middle of nowhere, tryin to get it out. Then National Lead moved the whole town up the road ten miles in the 1960s. This is what' s left."

"It's like artifacts," she said.

"Yeah, it is."

We smoked a cigarette and started on another beer. The beer was so cold in the summer heat, especially with the leather still on.

"I was sorry about your Mom."

"Thanks Jack. She was 90. There wasn't too much left."

"Did your sister come back for it?"

"I knew you'd ask."

"I knew you'd know."

She smiled. "No, she sent a religious card that she was busy with a youth group devoted to the Book of Mark."

"Jesus, what shit."

"And she told me she'd married the minister."

I didn't have words. Then Amanda said, "don't mourn her Jack. She's a lot like my mother was at the end. Not much left."

"You want another beer?"

"Sure."

"One more, then we'll head back."

As we drank, we edged our way back to the bike, a small array of near collapsed wooden shacks to our right. I took a long drink and I thought about it first. Then I said it.

"Did you ever think about us bein' more regular?"

"I've thought about it. I don't know. We're together for what we lost."

"And we do have a bit of fuckin' fun."

"That we do Jack."

"Now we gotta ride."

"Maybe we leave it the way it is now. Fun, no heavy lifting. I do look forward to seeing you though."

"I do too."

"You disappointed?"

"No, you're probably right. Could ruin the good parts of it."

"Could."

I started the bike and gave it juice. We started to pack up.

"My mother left me some money."

"I thought the home got it."

"Most of it."

"How much?"

"$3500.00"

"That aint' nothin. What you gonna do with it?"

"Maybe take a trip. I don't ever get out of town. Maybe to Maine."

"Nice."

"The bike would get us there?"

I smiled.

"The bike's in good shape," I said.

"Maybe in the fall."

"That sounds good."

We pulled out of Tahawus, the so called Lower Works and turned towards civilization. She was hanging on to my waist and I was taking it easy. We could talk through the headphone system and I heard her say, "Jack, I gotta pee."

I pulled off and a minute later she came out of the woods.

"That's better."

"Let's hit the road Majestic."

"One minute," she said.

A few seconds later she approached me. She stared hard at me. There was a tear in her eye. She grabbed my neck with both hands and kissed me hard.

THE SHAFT

The Clark twins showed us how to do it and we never gave it a second thought. We didn't understand fear or risk, what with being invincible and all. We were looking for fun, acting on dares and trying to come up with the next thing.

You simply threw the bikes down off 28N and followed the short path of sand and tall grass to the first bridge footing on the western side of the Hudson. At the base of the footing was a strategic rock about two feet tall. Lonnie and Don Clark were a couple of years older and taller. They could climb the concrete footing without stepping on the rock. But they showed us how to stand on it and jump upwards a foot or so and catch the base of our rib cages on the top shelf of the footing. From there you just scrapped your way up, until both legs were on top.

We both smiled a little to each other when we got up there, afraid I suppose that we might miss it in front of Lonnie and Don and publicly be deemed pussies for all time.

After getting up there that first time, Hutch and I brushed some of the gravel from our pants and began to study the underside of the bridge. There was a second footing, only ten feet or so away and it was a good test. The iron beams were painted rust red and the key was to take a few quick steps across the beam until you could reach one of the angled vertical posts. The vertical posts ran across the breadth of the bridge's undercarriage as diagonal support beams between the lateral beams.

Hutch went first. He made it look easy. Plus, right there we were only about 10 feet high, so a mistake was not a huge deal. I stepped across the beam, advancing from the footing toward the second footing and ultimately the river. I walked gingerly right to the middle and then paused. I took my eyes off the beam and made quick eye contact with Hutch.

"It's no prob," I said as much to myself as Hutch.

"No prob," Hutch said. "Come on, we'll keep going."

The horizontal under beams of the bridge ran across about three hundred yards of river at about thirty feet in the air. Each strand was ten quick steps to a post, hands free until you landed. Thirty feet doesn't seem like a lot, but in August in North Creek, the river was running at a depth of less than two feet. If you screwed up, it was going to hurt bad.

The Clark boys were halfway across the river when we caught up with them. It felt funny when a pulp truck or a truck coming from the mines crossed on the asphalt twenty feet above us. The whole bridge trembled. You held on for a minute, rode it out and then laughed a little.

Lonnie Clark was the best at it. He was like a circus performer. He never even held on to the vertical posts and sometimes took a few steps backward or jumped in the air. Lonnie was the blond with freckles. Don was the dirtier blond without.

There was no place to get down on the east side. So, after some talk about a girl who was thought to be a slut and the Clark brother's shared cigarette, we headed back. The water was so low that you could see the river rocks on the bottom. When we got back to the exact center, Lonnie did something crazy. He stepped slowly across the girder until he was exactly five feet either direction from a vertical post. He stopped dead in his tracks. He didn't say anything but you could feel something was about to happen. He flexed his legs, bent his knees slightly and checked his footing. When he was ready he jumped straight up in the air and spun 360 degrees, landing back on the crossing beam high above the shallow water. He landed square but then got careless. His momentum kept rotating him even though he was no longer in the air. He started to stumble.

"Jesus Lonnie, just sit down," Don said.

"I'm alright. I got this," Lonnie shot back.

With that he cautiously adjusted his balance and walked toward the next post. He reached out to stabilize himself and then remembered me and Hutch were watching.

"Fuck it," he said under his breath and walked right by the post without touching it.

I turned to Hutch and said simply, "That is the ballsiest thing I've ever seen."

Hutch didn't reply for a second. I think he was lost in the moment until he shook it off.

"Yes it sure was," Hutch agreed.

* * *

We went back four days later. We took Tunk Wilkins with us, but the Clark boys were elsewhere. Tunk was almost two years younger than us. He was to us as we were to Lonnie and Don. We knew he would be blown away. Looking back, it was a summer that seemed like it would never end. Tunk was short and a little odd looking. It didn't help that his parents ran the local funeral home. He was probably just over four feet tall. His hair was sandy brown and by late summer his tan seemed almost permanent. He had large, soft freckles on his face. It was about this time someone named him Wheat Thin and for a few years it stuck. Tunk aka Wheat Thin lost a grandfather in the war. Though he was small, he was agile, wiry and able to do things Hutch and I couldn't imagine. That was part of the reason for showing it to him. That and feeling like big shits as the twins had. We knew in advance Wheat Thin would love this.

He was, it turned out, what my late father- in -law referred to as a spider monkey. He ran toward the first concrete footing and used his forward momentum to scramble straight up the side without even using the stone.

"Hold up Wheat Thin until we get up there with you," I yelled.

He didn't want to wait for us. As Hutch and I struggled to the top of the footing Wheat Thin cried out in amazement, "This is just awesome."

Hutch and I were older and wiser and we guided Wheat Thin across the first girder, leading to the second footing and then the river. A few minutes later Wheat Thin laid down like an army commando and began mimicking the sound of rattling machine gun fire as he crawled out over the river, as if under enemy attack.

Hutch said casually to me, "We seem to have brought GI Joe's little brother to the bridge."

We decided to stop at the halfway point and sit on the beam and watch the river go slowly by.

"It's even shallower than last week," I said.

"Do you think a fall would definitely kill you at this height," Hutch asked.

"Make you wish you were dead anyways," I said.

"That's for sure."

"Remember four or five years ago when we had the flood," I asked.

Hutch nodded.

"They say one of the Hyde boys jumped from the road into the river."

"He lived," Wheat Thin added. "I saw him at the hardware two weeks ago."

"He lived cause the river was cresting over sixteen feet," I said.

"He had friends downstream with a rope out across the river that they used to fish him out as he flew by," Hutch explained.

"I don't think a fall would kill you, but it'd break both your legs for sure," our younger friend theorized.

Hutch couldn't resist adding, "You'd sure be a cracked Wheat Thin though."

After a few minutes we headed back, Hutch in the lead, me in the middle and Wheat Thin bringing up the rear. I yelled up to Hutch and asked whether he had bought the new Foreigner album. He said he was gonna, maybe next week.

"Why are they foreigner," Wheat Thin asked.

"Some of ' em are English, some are American, so the band doesn't have a home country," I explained.

"You see the cover," Hutch asked.

"Yeah, they're in long coats waiting for a train."

"Maybe they'll play Saratoga," Hutch said.

"I'd go," Wheat Thin said.

"Not without your mother Wheat Thin," Hutch said.

"Momma Thin," I joked.

This really pissed Wheat Thin off.

As if to prove himself, the angry four foot tall spider monkey started climbing one of the angled vertical supports. Before Hutch or I could even react, Wheat Thin was directly above our heads, by a solid ten or twelve feet.

"You fall from up there, Wheat Thin and you'll definitely be dead."
I said,

"You should see what I can see. Right down the old rail tracks to
the station."

"Climb on down Wheat Thin," Hutch said quietly.

"Wait a minute, I can see other shit I never seen before."

Hutch and I both knew he said shit to impress us. It was probably the
only time he said the word out loud.

"I aint' no pussy," Wheat Thin said.

"Didn't ever accuse you of it," I replied.

"What's that," he said and shimmied a foot or so higher.

"What do you see now Wheat Thin," Hutch asked.

"Across the tracks, it's all covered up with brush, can hardly make it
out, but there's an old mine shaft over there."

"Climb on down and we'll have a look," I said.

And finally, slowly and carefully, Wheat Thin eased his way down
the vertical beam, his anger overcome by the chance of exploring an actual
mine shaft.

* * *

The three of us waded through brush, small pieces of garbage and any
number of pricker bushes, drawing blood on each of our legs. Whatever
Wheat Thin had seen, hadn't been seen by anyone else in a long time. I
pushed through a final dense section of messy undergrowth and there it
was.

48

"I'll be damned," I said. "It's an old mine shaft."

Hutch pointed to the ground where there were the remains of an old conveyor belt apparently emerging from the mine shaft and pointed toward the railroad tracks. The front of the shaft had been boarded shut but with little effort Hutch and I were able to pull the mostly rotted wood out of the door frame and open the door. Looking in the opening, it was apparent that the conveyor line continued into the shaft. The opening itself was about twelve feet wide and the shaft seemed to descend gradually into the ground. The building that covered the shaft was a concrete triangle or wedge that seemed to have pierced the earth. Even the roof itself, which descended front to back at a 45 degree angle from the back was made of concrete.

"We goin' in," Wheat Thin asked, with perhaps a bit too much enthusiasm.

"Does a bear shit in the woods Wheat Thin," Hutch said.

Hutch had said shit before.

Hutch and I took a few cautious steps into the opening. It became dark rapidly. Hutch suggested we keep a hand on what was left of the conveyor belt to guide us where possible. That made good sense. We'd taken ten steps in, quickly descending below ground, when we couldn't see each other. We talked about nonsense things just to help chart our locality. To our surprise, it was getting colder.

Wheat Thin had had enough.

"I'm going back," he said.

"Actually, I don't think we should go any further," I said.

It was the first and one of the only times in my life I experienced absolute darkness and it was very disconcerting.

We all turned 180 degrees in the same rough motion. I moved my leg laterally until it touched the conveyor for guidance and we started to climb out. Eventually we climbed high enough so the opening was visible and each of us began to calm down.

We stood outside for a few minutes pondering the shaft, the rail line and the darkness. Hutch was the first to speak. "If we do this we're going to need light."

"That's for damn sure," I said.

"I got a friend," Wheat Thin said excitedly. "You guy's know him. T.O. His family's into camping and maybe he could get a hand on a couple of their new lanterns."

"Isn't he a little young," I said, not really expecting a reply.

"He ain't young, he's in my grade," Wheat Thin said.

"That reassuring," Hutch said.

* * *

The next afternoon we arrived at the shaft at noon. I don't remember how but Don and Lonnie rejoined Hutch and I. Wheat Thin arrived alone, followed by his friend T.O., silently carrying two battery powered lanterns he had lifted from his parents RV. Don looked at Wheat Thin and T.O. with complete disdain.

"Who are the two kids," Don asked.

"Without them we don't have light," I explained. "And wait and see Don, we're going to need light bad."

T.O. shyly handed one of the lanterns to Don and his twin Lonnie said, "Let's just do this thing."

We turned the lanterns on outside and it was such a clear, bright and sunny day we couldn't even be sure the bulbs were lit. The Clarks stepped into the shaft first with Hutch explaining they would need to use the conveyor belt as a guide. At first we all just walked in with no particular plan. Once underground, the concrete walls and ceiling were dirty and teeming with droplets of moisture. It had the feeling of having just rediscovered a lost war bunker.

We all stayed along the conveyor belt and quickly got beyond the point where Hutch, Wheat Thin and I had freaked out a day ago. The lanterns changed the descent. About sixty feet in I wished I had worn a sweat shirt. This was a place that had never seen the sun. We were probably only thirty feet below ground when the shaft narrowed and the decline became less steep. Even the twins were serious and quiet. We were likely in a place where no one had been for decades. The shaft became still more narrow, just wide enough for us to pass beside the conveyor. The good news was that the narrowness made the lanterns even more effective. The narrow passage continued another twenty feet. I heard Don ask Lonnie, "Do your feet feel funny?" And with that I reached down to touch the floor next to the conveyor.

"It's ice," I said.

"Ice and it's the fucking end of July," Don said.

"It's not just ice, it's thick as hell. Feels like the whole area flooded and has been frozen over for decades," Don added.

"Ice in July," Hutch said.

Up ahead it became apparent that something was about to change. The six of us stepped from the narrow tunnel into a wide, concrete loading area. The ceiling was high enough that we couldn't see it and though the conveyor extended to the center of the room, the room itself was more than sixty feet wide.

"The lanterns aren't worth squat here," Don said.

"You wouldn't like the alternative Don," I told him. "When we were down there the first time we couldn't even see each other's eyes."

"I get it, I get it."

After quietly walking a few more steps Lonnie asked, "So what do we do, just keep going?"

"Yeah, we try to find the end of this area, then maybe we'll know where we are," Don said.

Then something terrible happened. From nearly absolute silence we started to hear screeching and then a dull roar of fluttering wings as dozens of bats descended on us from above. We were all in the same boat, helplessly raising our arms to our faces to try to protect ourselves from the onslaught.

Wheat Thin and T.O. hadn't spoken out loud since we entered the large room and began walking across it on the floor of ice. One of the bats brushed up against T.O. and he screamed, "Make them go away."

As T.O. flailed his arms to fend off the bat army, he lost his grip on the lantern and it sailed across the room, shattering against a concrete wall.

"You're a fucking idiot kid," Don said.

"I want to go home," Wheat Thin said.

"Then go," Don answered.

Lonnie finally intervened. "Look, it's probably going to be easier to get out once we find the far wall than to try to turn around and go back."

Everyone mumbled agreement. T.O. quickly pulled his t shirt to his eyes and wiped away the tears. With one lantern we continued slowly across the room along the belt line in search of the far wall and possibly an exit.

* * *

We knew we had to be close to something, when abruptly the conveyor ended at a concrete and iron barrier that looked like a large book end. Don was carrying the one lantern and moving slowly and carefully, knowing all too well the shape we'd be in if we lost the last light. He and Lonnie literally ran into the wall at the same moment, both letting out a slow yelp of surprise.

Lonnie spoke first.

"Now what Don? Shine that lantern up there, I don't see no door, just a fifty foot high concrete wall."

Hutch, who would one day find his calling as a mechanical engineer many miles from his hometown, had a very practical side.

"Look, they're bringing shit in on the conveyor, probably rock or something. They bring it all the way down here. Not to leave it here, but to take it someplace else. There had to be men unloading it. They would need a way up at the end of the day."

"You're right," Don said.

"The wall's about sixty feet wide," Hutch went on. "It's going to be dark and it's going to be scary, but there's six of us. Let's each of us take a ten foot stretch and feel our way around."

Don set the lantern down carefully. Each of us slowly spread across the wall and claimed a ten foot search area. It was so dark I never saw the wall. Just rammed into it. We slowly, methodically and blindly slid our hands across the wall and as we found nothing, moved a few feet to the side.

It was actually feeling pretty hopeless. I think all of us were thinking we would likely have to turn around, recross the ice, enter the narrow part of the shaft and attempt to retrace our steps back to daylight. I had covered ten feet, maybe a little more. I heard Hutch mumble under his breath, "this ain't good." I couldn't even see any of the others and the lantern seemed as far away as a distant lighthouse would to a ship lost at sea.

When it felt totally hopeless and several of us were reassembling near the lantern, we all heard Wheat Thin scream out from a far corner near the right side of the room.

"Hey," Wheat Thin yelled.

"Hey what," Lonnie asked.

"I think I found a ladder," Wheat Thin said.

We all moved quickly, following Wheat Thin's voice and in his haste to see what had been found, Don kicked the second lantern over and left the six of us in complete darkness, following the sound of Wheat Thin's voice to the mythical ladder which now seemed likely to be our only way out.

"Guess we're even T.O.," Don said.

"Sure are," T.O. said.

"Keep talking Wheat Thin, it's the only way we're going to find you," Hutch said.

* * *

We huddled around the base of the ladder. It was made of steel and appeared to be bolted into the concrete wall. Some of the first rungs were bent but none of them were broken.

It felt like Don was our de facto leader and after killing the second lantern and owning it to T.O. we seemed to coalesce as a group. I had something to say to Don and after a couple of stammers I spit it out.

"Look, I know you and Lonnie are the big shits here and you're in charge and headed into high school and all that."

"Yeah, so what," Don said.

"Well it's about Wheat Thin. I ain't never seen anybody who can climb like him. Sure he's young, but he's also the lightest of all of us. I think he needs to go ahead of us. Look straight up there Don. I mean, way up. It almost looks like there may be light up there. I say Wheat Thin leads us out."

"I can climb anything Don," Wheat Thin volunteered.

"Then start climbing Wheat Thin, and if we get to the top and get the fuck out of here, maybe I'll even call you Tunk."

"Deal," Wheat Thin said, as he put his foot lightly on the first rung.

"No bullshit. Go up slow and careful," Don said.

"Right," Wheat Thin responded.

"Go up eight to ten steps, turn back to me and say, "all good"," Don said.

"Only two on the ladder. Once he's up, T.O. leads for Lonnie and you two work it out between yourselves. If anything goes totally wrong, we only lose two," Don said.

"And whoever is left is trapped down here," Hutch pointed out.

"Beats falling to your death if those fifty year old bolts pull out of the concrete," Don said.

Now ten steps up, Wheat Thin was having little difficulty.

"All good," he called to Don and Don slowly started up the ladder.

A minute or so later Wheat Thin shouted back down, "all good."

The four of us were left at the ladder's base to watch the other two disappear into the blackness. Occasionally we would hear another, "all good." A few minutes later we heard an excited Wheat Thin scream back down.

"Broken rung. Eight above where you are now. Watch out, it's sharp as a knife."

"Got it," Don replied.

A moment later he confirmed he was over the broken rung. Don was the first to have an idea of where they were coming out.

"You see anything yet Wheat Thin."

"A lot of light now. I'm almost to the top."

"I think we're coming up in the main part of that boarded up plant from the war," Don said.

"I think you're right," Wheat Thin agreed.

A moment later Wheat Thin called back down.

"The top is sketchy. The bolts in the last strand are pulling out of the wall. Go up it quick." Then a few seconds later, "I'm out."

Wheat Thin looked around the room, which had apparently been a storage area. There was broken glass everywhere. Empty boxes and old equipment with no discernable purpose lined one wall. As his eyes finally adjusted to the light, he heard Don come off the last step.

"How high do you figure we climbed?"

"Nearly sixty feet I guess."

"That's a lot."

"Yes it is."

Don laid down on the floor and called to the others.

"Send up T.O.," he yelled.

Then Don extended a hand to Wheat Thin and as they shook hands, he said, "Tunk, you done real good."

* * *

I was the last one up. Hutch was seven to eight steps above me. He was two rungs from the top when thee corroded bolts on both sides pulled out of the ancient concrete. All at once the top strand of the ladder pulled free from the wall and began falling backwards. Don saw it from above. He dove across the floor and barely got a hand on the top rung. He screamed at Lonnie to grab his legs so he didn't go over with us.

Lonnie got ahold of him and Don got a firmer grip on the ladder. Wheat Thin grabbed Don's other leg and they pulled him backwards while he held the ladder. This had the effect of returning the top section of ladder to its original placement, absent anything to secure it. I screamed at Hutch, "Climb fast while they hold it."

I didn't have to ask twice. He took another step up and dove the last few feet, landing firmly on the mill floor with the announcement made to no one in particular that he had just about pissed himself.

And there I stood, eight rungs from the top with Don literally holding my life in his hands. He spoke quickly to me, almost in a hiss.

"Come up slow and soft and lean into the wall as much as you can. It takes the pressure off my hands. And don't jump when you get close, I almost lost you when Hutch jumped off."

Strangely enough, I wasn't freaked out. It was the first time in my life a character trait that would be of consequence in a distant legal career presented itself. I was oddly calm, task oriented, feeling I had it. I began climbing slowly. Each time I cleared one rung, I paused and leaned in hard to give Don a break. A few moments later I stepped over the precipice and Don released the ladder. We all stood in complete silence as we heard the top ten feet of ladder crash its way down the sixty foot drop, clattering against the concrete wall.

None of us spoke for awhile. Don broke the silence.

"That was very nearly you Taylor."

"I'm not going to think about it," I said.

We sort of huddled together. A few high fives were exchanged. Someone mentioned that I was the last person who would ever climb out of the shaft. Somehow that was a funny way for me to think about it. My calm trance was wearing off and I was trying hard to hide from the others that my entire upper body was trembling. I stuck my hands in my front pockets to hide the shaking. Wheat Thin slapped my back.

"In a pinch, you climb almost as good as me," he said.

* * *

Eight years later... Dear God, what a difference between twelve and twenty. I was quiet, but cocky in my own intellectual way. I didn't think I knew everything. I did.

I had double majored in economics and history. The latter was my love. The former what my old man explained might one day make a mortgage payment. As smart as I was, I had no idea what he was talking about.

My college was small and far upstate. It has been a den of liberalism during the Nixon years and extremely vocal in the anti- war movement. A few years later that scent was still in the air. My American history lecture might have been about a new concept called workplace democracy but the fuel for the professor was still Tet, Nixon, the Draft and a disparate wealth system that sent young boys to the infantry while the elite somehow sheltered in the Eastern Ivy League.

My girlfriend was a sociology major with a minor in economics. She was smart but probably liked weed too much. On the one hand she eagerly looked forward to a January term comparing the economy of rural West Virginia to the Adirondacks. On the other hand, she cunningly planned her last ten days of the term to be a field study in the Adirondacks conveniently near my aging parents who still lived near North Creek. My job was to find a J term project that would free me up to jointly coast through that part of winter, ski a bit, party more and write a paper about society of some sort.

Ahhh, J Term. My college still clung to the once trendy 4- 1-4 curriculum, meaning the middle month, wedged between two regular semesters, was an opportunity for extreme experimental learning, both on and off campus. Some of the classic courses: Write the American Novel; The Fiction of Faulkner; The Beatles in Culture. My choice, of course made on the final day to pick, was the following:

The Tradition of Oral History – An introduction to the collection and evaluation of oral personal journeys. The course will first immerse students in the work of Studs Terkel, including the methodology of collecting traditions. The course will culminate with a student field experience requiring students to engage in an approved oral documentation of a local or regional personality associated with an event, time or place of historical consequence.

Bingo, I thought. Two weeks on campus and two weeks skiing Gore, drinking Bud Lights and sharing a few joints with Angela, who surely by then would have solved the issue of rural economic disparity in an American capitalistic economy.

A few weeks later, as J- Term began, my well set plan developed a problem. The oral history class was tiny and it was not possible for me to hide. By the end of the first week I was the only student to not have an approved oral history project. I had thrown out a half dozen ideas that were unworkable and largely inconsistent with drinking, skiing and Angela. It was in a conversation on the phone with my old man that the idea struck me. He said, "You're looking too hard."

I told him I had looked so hard I couldn't think. I was so desperate I was toying with dropping the course altogether. In that same conversation, my father had said, "Think of one thing that punched you in the gut. Does that tie to history? If it does, you've got a topic, but by the way, you still don't have a job."

And of course the obvious came to me as if it had been hovering just above me all along. The National Lead titanium loading facility in North Creek. Yes, something had punched me in the gut at that place but by God it was also a place tied to events of historic consequence.

"Dad, is there anybody still alive who worked at the plant near the river along the train tracks?"

"The National Lead building?"

"Yeah, that's it."

"It ran in the forties. I'm sure there's people left who worked there." After a brief pause, he added, "Will Thompson is around, I saw him last week. He's older but still sharp. He was a young man then, but I think he helped run the plant."

"Then Will's my guy," I said.

"And when you finish with Will, take two minutes and tell me where you're headed year after next."

"Will do Dad. Love you. Gotta go."

* * *

Nine days later, Studs Terkel Jr. was in Downtown North Creek, interviewing one Will Thompson over two cups of piping hot black coffee. The diner was called "The Red Diner." It made sense, the building being both red and a diner. My interview questions had been carefully scrutinized by my professor and I was armed with a brand new Panasonic cassette recorder and extra double A batteries just in case.

Will started talking without questions.

"They say your father's sick."

"He's lost a lot of weight, but I think it could be more healthy long term."

"Nothing else going on?"

"No, normal stuff in your sixties."

"Say no more, I was there fifteen years ago."

"You look good. Do you mind me asking how old you are?"

I slyly turned the tape recorder on.

"Seventy- Four last month. You give your old man my best. This community can't afford to lose a man like him. Now you need to learn about titanium, correct?"

I left the tape on, forgot my prepared questions and just listened.

"I should have served, would have served, but the Japs got my big brother. He arrived in Manila five days before the Japs took the airport. two days later the island fell. In a way he was lucky. He took a bullet in the head and was gone instantly. A classmate of mine was there too. Survived Manila to be in a prison boat and the Bataan Death March. Sometimes dying's not so bad. That's the history you ought to write. But we need to talk about titanium, right?

"So the Army wouldn't take me. My brother was dead. It was a deal breaker at that time in the war. And my parents weren't well anyway. So I stayed home and took the job with National Lead. First, in Newcomb where the mine is, but then at the loading plant in North Creek.

"Durant built the line. He was going to get rich off the Adirondacks. You know Durant, right? Well, he went belly up. Most people seem to in the Adirondacks. Sold the line to his boy, William West and later Delaware and Hudson. Anyway, he got the line two miles north of North Creek but no further. So come the war, you got product in the ground in Newcomb thirty miles north. You got all the pork on earth but no way to get it to market.

"So they truck it. Truck the ore from 1941 to June of 1944. I came on in 1943. Got promoted quick because I was young, had half a brain and there were almost no men. End of 1943 I was assistant plant manager of the North Creek loading operation. The tracks were going to be extended to Newcomb but it was going to take time.

"Titanium made paint and a half dozen other things the war needed. So they trucked it from Newcomb. Tahawus actually. It was Moser Trucking LTD to the North Creek plant. The product went out of the truck bed and onto conveyor belts. There were belts all around the outside of the building. My lady at the time had a joke about the belts. She said the building looked like it wore its underwear on the outside.

"So the product moved off the trucks and onto the belts until it hit the drop. The drop was way in the back of the building, behind our offices and a shop area. It dropped off the conveyor system straight down fifty feet or so. Down there was another conveyor system and a half dozen men reloaded the product.

"The second conveyor system was below ground. Once the belts were loaded in the drop the belts began to pull the product out of the drop and up towards daylight. It took awhile. I didn't work much in the drop but I can tell you it was always cold and wet down there. Seemed like the men down there were sick half the time.

"The ore worked its way on the belt up through a narrow shaft, gaining a few feet in elevation every few yards or so. When it finally emerged into daylight, the belt system carried it higher up still into the conveyor building. Only one man up there. Best job on the crew. You watched the product come up and into the building some twenty feet above land and turn quickly at a right angle. After a few feet more the product would then be dropped through a hole in the floor of the building into a waiting freight car.

"Part of the conveyor building is still there. I'll walk out if you want. I won't take you down in the shaft though. That was dicey twenty years ago. So by 1944 they could finally run a train to Tahawus and our operation slowly went downhill.

"In our prime though, Jesus in our prime, you'd never know it to look at that site but we could run four lines of rail rack under the conveyor building. There were twenty four men there full time. We could load upwards of sixteen hundred tons of ore in a single day. In my mind I get the train to Newcomb but I don't think they ever matched our capacity until years after Hitler and Tojo were dead meat.

"Now I got one question for you son."

"Shoot."

"What a funny thing to write a college paper on. What the hell?"

"It always struck my interest. I played there when I was a kid," I explained.

"Not a good place to be playin.'"

"Looking back, no. But you know, young and dumb."

"I can't remember back to young. But you stay away from there now. Something bad could happen there. It's even too dangerous to take pictures."

* * *

Don Clark led us around the back portion of the abandoned plant.

"We've come this far, might as well take the tour," he said.

Wheat Thin and T.O. looked scared shitless but they had little choice but to follow. Gradually we were making our way to the front of the building. There was an old newspaper next to a pile of grease rags. The headline from September of 1951 read, "Senator McCarthy Hunts Reds in Hollywood." I dropped the paper and wiped my hands on my jeans.

Don and Lonnie were now out of the equipment room and moving toward the front of the building. No one spoke out loud and by then all of us were anxious to see a doorway that might pass us back through to our bikes, school shopping and a hot dinner.

Don's right hand quickly shot in the air. Lonnie, immediately behind him, turned to the rest of us and whispered, "Quiet, Don thinks he hears something."

Don's advance continued but at a slower, cautious pace. Advancing into a hallway that led to the front of the plant, I thought I heard something too. It was not loud but a quiet thumping, like something bumping against the wall in one of the outer rooms. As I walked a few more steps the noise became louder. I thought perhaps a small animal had become trapped and was persistently bashing the wall trying to get out.

Now Lonnie was standing next to Don and they had stopped walking. Instead of continuing down the hallway, they turned right into what had probably been Will Thompson's old office, as I would learn years later. It was a smart move. They could peek through the deteriorating walls and have a safe look into the next room without advancing. The thumping sound of wood on wood was now joined by a quieter sound of springs squeaking. The twins looked through the same horizontal wall crack and then turned immediately to each other, their eyes wide open in complete awe.

"There's a man and a woman in there on an old cot," Don whispered.

"What are they doing," Hutch whispered.

"It."

"What?"

"They're doing it right there right now."

The twins were ready for another look. T.O. and Wheat Thin were both confused and terrified. Hutch and I both approached another horizontal crack in the wall and looked. The man was on top of the woman and every time he pushed down it slammed the metal headboard of the cot into the wall. The woman couldn't even be seen except for the side of her leg.

"What do we do now," Hutch whispered.

"I want to go home," T.O. said softly and then added, "really bad."

Lonnie looked back through the wall. He whispered to his brother, "I can see the woman's face now. She's crying."

Each of us heard her cry and then loudly sob. The sob was muffled when the man put his hand over her mouth. Sure as anything we heard him warn her.

"Shut the fuck up or I won't let you breath anymore."

"This is not right," Lonnie said.

Lonnie and Don looked at each other without speaking. Don nodded once and Lonnie nodded in return. A moment later they launched into the room and Don plowed into the man with all the force he could muster. The naked man was thrown from the cot and for a moment sat disoriented on the plant floor. Hutch and I edged into the room. We gathered the woman's clothes and handed them to her as she tried to hide herself under a dirty sheet on the cot.

"Get dressed and get out," I said.

She was crying much harder now.

"Thank you. Thank you," she said.

As she dressed, Hutch and I turned away to give her privacy, which somehow seemed an odd consideration after what we had already witnessed. The naked man got to his feet and moved on Don and Lonnie together. First, he punched Don hard on the side of the head, literally leveling him. The man said, "you dumb sons of bitches, I'll kill you both." With that he bodily drove Lonnie to the floor and began choking him. The man was too much for the twins together and was easily able to overpower them, one by one.

"We got to do something Hutch," I said.

As the two of us moved towards the man, Don was trying to get up and get his wits about him. The woman had slipped out a side door.

"He's going to kill Lonnie," I said.

The man was now violently shaking Lonnie as he choked him, as if to say, "there, finish the job." It was shadowy, but in the dark I saw a movement behind Don.

An instant later, little T.O. appeared behind the man and, holding a large chunk of jagged cinderblock, screamed loudly, "Get the fuck off Lonnie."

As T.O. did this he slammed the block down on the man's skull. Not once but in a spasm of eight or more blows, crushing his head. A missed blow shattering into the back of the man's neck.

In a few seconds it was over. The man rolled off Lonnie and was struggling for air and coughing up blood. T.O. followed the man to the floor and beat him again with the block. Only when Don got ahold of him did he relent.

"It's alright T.O. It's all over," Don said.

With that, T.O. dropped the block and collapsed on the floor crying. Wheat Thin sat next to him with his arm around him. The man lay very dead, the back of his skull a mess of blood, bone and brain tissue.

Everyone was silent again except for T.O.'s crying. Lonnie stepped towards T.O. and said, "Buddy you saved my life."

To this proclamation T.O. smiled slightly as he kept crying. Then he pointed quizzically to the man he had just beaten to death and said, " How does that happen?"

"I noticed it too," Don said.

"How can a dead guy have a boner," Lonnie asked.

After a bit of a pause, Wheat Thin said, "You guys know my father runs the funeral home, right?"

"Yeah," they all acknowledged.

"Well you pick things up. They call that angel lust. I heard my father tell my mother about a man that had it after he hanged himself."

"Aren't you a fountain of information Wheat Thin," Hutch said.

* * *

We sat inside alone for another few minutes until we came to an agreement we could all stand by. We called it "Pentagon" because it had five walls. The walls went as follows:

One: Don and Lonnie had a near death fight over a girl. This would explain the bruising on Lonnie's neck and the slight petechial hemorrhaging or blood that appeared in his eyes as the vessels had begun to burst. Don would take whatever punishment his father gave him and shut up.

Two: They would put some clothes on the body, boner and all, and shove it under the cot.

Three: Taylor and Hutch would nail shut the entrance to the shaft and steal a post it sign from another property to be placed on the front of the doorway.

Four: None of them would ever go in or near the former National Lead Titanium transport facility again.

Five: They would never speak of it again. Not to anyone else and not to each other.

We all shook hands after the dead man was pushed under the cot. "Pentagon," I said.

"Pentagon," everyone replied.

Don went out first and surveyed 28N. It was clear. Hutch was last out and shut the door. We found our bikes where we had dumped them five hours before.

I looked at Hutch and said, "Jesus."

After considerable thought, Hutch replied ," Yup,"

And so we went back to dinner with our families and perhaps some late night baseball on a new color T.V. Pentagon was effective. T.O. seemed quieter after it all but what the hell. Our five part plan protected a day we were all happy to forget. Pentagon. The only one who ever violated its terms was me.

* * *

What is twenty four years? Twenty Four years means most of us saw it online and not in a print news story that was part of a paper a local kid might have slung in the yard. Late thirties for me, new partner in a growing firm, a toddler upstairs getting settled in by my wife. Habit made me click on the news sources, the same every time. CNN, Reuters, Post Star. And then I saw the headline.

Mystery in North Creek

Skeletal remains found in an abandoned World War II shipping facility have created a significant mystery for state and local law enforcement officials.

The body of a male subject was found Wednesday among interior building rubble at the former National Lead titanium facility in North Creek. The as yet unidentified individual remains will be the subject of an autopsy to be conducted at the New York State Police lab in Albany.

The age and date of death of decedent were unavailable at press time.

Local authorities indicated that the discovery does not seem related to any current missing persons reports.

I was about to call Hutch, now working in Saratoga County as a mechanical engineer and then I remembered. Pentagon.

* * *

I've stopped believing in coincidences. It surely couldn't have been pure happenstance that Hutch and his kids were eating pumpkin ginger-bread at Café Sarah's when I went in for an Americano en route to visiting my elderly mother in North Creek. Life and time had gotten away from us. His two girls must have been ten and twelve years old. He was probably visiting his mother as well.

I was certainly bigger in the mid section and my hair was peppered gray. Hutch on the other hand seemed not to have aged.

We shook hands, exchanged greetings and he made his girls say hello. They awkwardly complied and then asked if they could go outside. I sat down next to him and he handed me a newspaper.

"I assume you saw this," Hutch said.

"Read it online at 5 a.m."

"Yeah, I don't sleep either."

"We should go down there again. At least to the bridge."

"I'm in, but I'll leave the girls with Helen. I don't want them to know about all of the stupid shit we used to do."

Hutch went to gather the girls and deposit them with his mother. I cashed out and drove down the road to see my mother. My father had been gone nearly ten years. My mother was a bit like Hutch, she didn't seem to age.

About an hour later, I found myself grappling with the first bridge abutment. I needed more than just the stepping stone to pull myself up. Only a firm boost from Hutch got me to the top. We both chuckled as I reached down to help Hutch up.

"We're fucking old," Hutch said.

"That we are," I said.

Slowly we walked across the first support girder towards the second footing.

"I don't remember it being so damned high," I said.

"Me either," Hutch said.

I paused and held tight to the first angled vertical girder. There had been a second article buried later in the paper. Authorities had concluded the remains found in the building were likely those of a homeless man who was killed when a portion of the former industrial plant collapsed on him as he slept.

"Let's go one more beam, at least we could say we got over the water."

"One more is all I've got in me," I said.

The next steps were perilous for me. It felt like the world was spinning but I made it to the next vertical girder and held on for dear life. Both Hutch and I were sweating a bit as we sat on the horizontal support beam, our feet dangling over the Hudson.

"God Taylor, can you believe that was twenty four years ago."

"I always wondered if the shaft door stayed boarded up all those years."

"I'm not checking."

"Me either."

"Lonnie's dead," Hutch asked.

"Yeah, four or five years ago. Motorcycle crash on the Northway. They said he was pretty drunk and his brother Don is doing hard time in state prison."

"At least Wheat Thin's still around."

"That boy was always cut out for mortuary studies. Still runs the family business in town," Hutch said.

"And where is T.O.," I asked.

"No one knows," Hutch said. "Left town after graduation and has never been seen or heard from again."

It was quiet for a moment. Soft, early evening at the end of a long, late summer day. The crickets were out, water bugs danced twenty feet below us.

"Hutch, I've got a confession."

"Oh Boy."

"I never told anyone this but I violated Pentagon, just a week after it happened."

"You telling me now? That would be a second violation."

"I ought to tell someone."

"Spit it out."

"It was a few days before school and it was still all I could think about. I came to the conclusion in my mind that Pentagon was a flawed plan. What we'd really made it look like was that someone was trying to hide a dead guy."

"So what did you do?"

"I went back through the side door that the girl had run out of. I waited until early dusk, enough light to get around without a flashlight but enough darkness for cover. I pulled him out from under the cot."

"Did he.....?"

"I couldn't tell."

"Continue."

"It was all I could do to lay him out on the bed. I put him on his stomach. The wound on his head was still an awful site. He was beginning to decompose and stiff with rigor mortis but I was able to make it look like he had been laying there. I found the stone T.O. had used and put it right next to his head. Then I went over near the side wall and loosened a board and found two other stones and threw it all on top of him. I don't know if you remember but there were shelves on some of the walls. I broke them and scattered them in the bed and all around the floor. Made the place look more fucked up than it had been, and then I snuck out. Over the years that part of the building took the brunt of rain and snow and gradually began to cave."

"You ever go to the county fair," Hutch asked.

"Once or twice, why?"

"I saw her there when I was in high school."

"The girl?"

"Yes, the girl. Actually the woman."

"Did she know you?"

"I think so. She was with another man and he was tipsy. She had the brownest, saddest eyes and as we passed each other, she kind of nodded and I nodded back."

"Who was she?"

"No idea."

"Back when I was in law school, first year of criminal law, you know they grind the hell out of you."

"Heard that."

"Anyways, we studied crime and the elements of crime and one day we read about something called 'accomplice after the fact.' I started to ask myself, was I one? Was I an accomplice after the fact when I went back and trashed the room and moved the body?"

"Don't look at me, I design municipal sewer systems."

"Well how could I be, if there had been no initial crime to assist for."

"You can't kick an extra point without a touchdown."

"Same idea, I guess."

We both stood up slowly and with great care.

"God, it's strange to be back, isn't it?"

"It sure the hell is."

"It's our hometown, we grew up right here and yet when I go in the store I don't know anyone. Everybody looks at me like I'm the foreigner and not them."

"I get that too."

We were quiet for a moment, both looking upriver, me asking myself, am I really remembering an event or really remembering a memory of a memory that is less acute each time.

"Do you remember Lonnie jumping up and spinning 360 degrees in the middle of the bridge," Hutch asked.

"He almost didn't land it," I said.

"Very true, but it sure was a ballsy thing to do," Hutch added.

Hutch bent down slightly and torqued his body as if he were thinking about repeating Lonnie's trick jump twenty four years later.

Gradually he stood straight up, smiled at me and said "Better not.

STARGAZER

Lenny Linden was sketchy from the get- go. There were the obvious things. He constantly reeked of stale cigarettes. At eighteen, he needed to start shaving but hadn't and his face was a patchwork of hairy tufts of untamed growth and clear areas where stubble refused to take root. He had dropped out of school a year before but was often seen on the south end of varsity field enjoying a Camel filter less cigarette and a competitive girls' field hockey game.

I suppose he came off as a lurker almost by definition, but there were other things, less obvious and only known to a few of us, which made his situation even more strange. He lived in a run- down clapboard ranch on Morton Street. Whether I was walking home from school or to my summer job, I passed the house with great frequency. My brother Barry, who also passed it often, advised me in no uncertain terms, "You stay the fuck away from those people, Ed. They're just not right."

Truthfully, I never saw any other Linden outside. At night, you might see the profile of family members through a window, that is if there were lights on. Barry said four people lived there: Lenny, Lenny's older parents and a grandmother who was apparently wheelchair bound. Only Lenny went outside.

How did they live like that? Did Lenny do the grocery shopping? There was an old Dodge pickup in the driveway with the front end on cinderblocks, so that wasn't going anywhere. Did they ever go to the doctor, or visit relatives? And what did Barry mean when he said they weren't right? I pressed him on it but all I got was, "some things are better left unsaid."

It's a good thing God doesn't give us a crystal ball that shows us how things are going to end up. I've thought of that a couple of times and I think it would make it impossible to live life. In the Summer of 1980, I was in a relationship that I thought would last forever. I had the newfound freedom of a driver's license and a 75' Super Beetle that would go one hundred miles on $2 worth of gas. I was accepted at my college of choice and Barry had moved out to take a job in Texas.

My folks were older and had long given up on curfews, domestic chores and rules that weren't going to be followed anyways. I had my own cash from a good job in Lake George and basically did what I wanted which was pretty much harmless. On a Friday night I might have $40 in my wallet, a six pack of Molson Golden on the floorboard and plans to pick up Leisha at 8 p.m. when her waitressing gig ended.

There was a Friday in early August that was quite typical. If I remember correctly, we had shopped for college clothes in Glens Falls before driving north to party with our friends. I had gassed up and beered up at Conway's Country Store and was pulling out of the parking area to get back on Route 28. I guess I wasn't thinking and wasn't as focused as I should have been. But also, he shouldn't have been walking on the side of the road at 10 p.m. in dark jeans and a black shirt.

Leisha saw him first. She screamed, "look out?"

I locked up the brakes and the little VW did all it could. It halted perhaps a foot, maybe two short of running over Lenny Linden walking alone up Route 28 carrying a bag of groceries.

He stared at us for a second, like when a deer freezes on the road in your head lights. Then, quite abruptly, he turned away as if nothing had happened and continued walking north.

"Jesus Christ," I muttered under my breath.

"We could have killed him," Leisha said.

"Well what the hell is he doing wandering the road in the middle of the night in black clothes?"

"Who was it?"

"Lenny fucking Linden," I said.

"Oh God," Leisha said. "My father says his old man is bad news. Said stay away from the whole tribe."

"Well, the tribe just about got one smaller."

I finally pulled back on the highway. We drank some beers later around a fire with our friends. My buddy Kenny had a new Kenwood car stereo with rear mounted speakers installed facing backwards. When he opened the back hatch of the Pinto, the sound was incredible. We talked about woofers and tweeters, college, a girl who had been killed in a car crash the summer before. On its face, it was a normal Friday in the rural Adirondacks.

But to be honest, both Leisha and I were spooked by the near collision with Lenny Linden. The idea that I could have killed him sunk in slowly, but for both of us, there was something more. There had a been a look of terror in Lenny's eyes that couldn't be explained. It wasn't just the near death experience, it was the sense that we had, for an instant, invaded his place, grabbed him by the collar and shook him into recognition before he turned to head home. He certainly had the look of fear, but he had another look too. He'd been found out.

As always, I stopped the Bug a mile from Leisha's house. We shared one more beer and kissed a bit.

"Do you think it's stupid," she asked.

"What?"

"Me wanting to apply to the same school as you next year."

"No, I think it's great, I want you to."

"It means we're going to stay together, right?"

"Right."

"What is it about that guy that still freaks me out?"

"The fact that he's a freak."

"My father said his old man did something bad in the war... in Vietnam."

"I hadn't heard that one," I stated. "Barry just said keep away at all costs."

"I can't say the name."

"What name?"

"Of the place."

"What place Leisha?"

"My Lai."

"Lenny's father is a baby killer?"

"My father says he either killed them or tried to stop it."

"Jesus."

"How would we know which?"

"We wouldn't...and we're not gonna, cause we're not asking."

And then she said the last thing I ever expected Leisha Thompson, my high school sweetheart of fifteen months to say, "Let's drive over by their house."

* * *

I pulled onto the shoulder of Morton Street, seventy five feet from the house. I quickly killed the engine and popped off the headlights.

"Why are we here," I asked.

"Why do none of them ever go outdoors?"

"It appears Lenny does everything. Even after hours grocery shopping."

"They might have starved if we killed him."

"Enough Leisha. He nearly killed himself."

"I'm getting out."

Before I could stop her, she had quietly opened the passenger door. She soundlessly pushed the door shut and started creeping toward the Linden house. I had no choice but to go after her. It was the last place on earth I wanted to be. Before getting out, I popped another beer, figuring what could it hurt and in the back of my mind acknowledging that, if things got weird, I could use it as a weapon.

When I reached Leisha she was in the side yard of the Linden house.

"Let's look in the windows," she said.

Having come this far, I had to admit I was kind of curious. The grass was wet with evening dew and the night peepers were loud enough to provide cover for our hesitant steps. Carefully, we peered into the closest window. There was a man, brown hair gone mostly gray, asleep in a lazy boy recliner while the tv blared an episode of "Dallas."

"Lenny's father," I whispered.

"Must be," Leisha said and then added, "Larry Linden."

In the kitchen behind the recliner a woman was hastily washing dishes while smoking a cigarette. Next to the black and white Zenith was a stand with black and white photos. The largest picture showed a man in the jungle, likely Larry, in combat fatigues and holding an M-16. Next to that were pictures of a very young Lenny, an older couple I didn't recognize, and a small picture in a gold wire frame of someone I did recognize. It was Valerie Lambert, a Sophomore, just one year behind Leisha. Must be a cousin, I thought.

"Seen enough," I asked.

"Let's go to the back."

"Let's go home."

"Just a few more steps."

While the bellowing voice of J.R. Ewing receded, I followed Leisha around to the back of the house. I thought I heard something, so I grabbed the back of her belt to slow her down. She glared at me for a moment, but then, she heard it too. It was a short, staccato light electrical pop. I held up my hand in a stop motion and raised my index finger as if to say, 'one minute.' I stepped around her to take the lead and we inched our way toward the rear corner of the house.

We crept closer to the back corner and stopped short when we heard the electrical noise again, this time with more clarity. It was a short, soft jolt, followed by silence and then the sound of an opening door. I stepped forward again, reached the back corner of the house and carefully turned toward the noise.

I quickly turned to Leisha, placing my index finger over my lips to urge silence. I moved enough so she too could look into the backyard. In the distance there was an outdoor light and it somehow emboldened us. Our end of the house was pitch black, which oddly made us feel more secure in our darkened veil. We edged forward. My foot- steps were cautious, each foot fall testing to make certain that the ground was solid beneath my feet. After a few more quiet advances my next step hit a solid obstruction and my foot did not even reach the ground. I signaled to Leisha to stop and in the darkness struggled to get my bearings.

To call it a deck was an exaggeration. There were four or five wood pallets lined up and drawn tight against the rear wall of the house. At the far end of this loose structure, more pallets had been stacked on top of the first layer creating an elevated area about eight by eight in size. About seven feet above the pallets hung a bare white light bulb swinging by its cord, throwing harsh illumination on an electric bug zapper that was hard at work.

Lenny was sitting on the elevated pallet in an old torn up lawn chair from the 1960s. Beside him was an old woman, probably in her nineties and sitting in a wheelchair. They were talking quietly together. I heard Lenny call her "grandma." Then I heard her speak.

"Southern sky," she said.

"Ok," Lenny said, and then gathering himself, stared straight upward into the heavens and began to speak. "The Summertime Triangle, with Vega shining brightly, Mars, Big Dipper, Sagittarius. Oh, and Scorpius."

"I feel I can see them," Grandma said.

Leisha shifted her feet, making the slightest sound. Lenny heard nothing but Grandma, who's hearing had become increasingly acute with the progression of her blinding glaucoma, turned in our direction. The raw light from the swinging bulb revealed a soft, round and ancient face looking blindly at us. Her eyes had no pupils and glowed across the yard in our direction as if the two orbitals had been replaced with cloudy, blue illuminated marbles.

Grandma turned slowly away from us and stared straight into the summertime sky. I finally exhaled and attempted to regain my composure.

"No Libra tonight," Grandma queried.

"I can't make it out," Lenny said.

The blind woman struggled to lift her right arm to point towards the sky.

"There, you see it now Lenny? There, beside Scorpius. Use the star wheel if it helps."

Lenny raised the star gazing tool to his eyes. What Grandma called the star wheel consisted of two small discs that rotated around a common pivot. The first disc was a star and constellation chart. The second disc overlayed the first and rotated around it with a small window to show parts of the chart. The overlay also contained dates and times. By rotating the top disc over the bottom, one could locate stars and clusters and identify their status as of particular dates and times.

"You're the only person I've ever heard call it a star wheel," Lenny said.

"I don't recall, what do they call it now?"

"A Planisphere."

"Oh yes, I remember now. Well, can you make it out," Grandma asked.

Lenny carefully turned the two cylinder star locator and then said, "I have it now, but only faintly."

"We moved here for the dark," Grandma said.

"You've told me that," Lenny answered.

"No bright artificial lights," Grandma said.

"No light pollution," Lenny added.

"Your grandfather always said the dark night of the Adirondacks was its fairest gift," Grandma said.

"That's a funny way to say it."

"That was your grandfather."

"I wish I had known him," Lenny said.

"In a way you surely do."

They paused and both stared upward.

"Take my hand Lenny."

"Yes Grandma."

"I know how much you do for us."

"It's nothing."

"It is though, I see it clearly. Remember, I'm blind. No artificial light."

Lenny chuckled at that.

"No light pollution for you Grandma."

"Did I ever tell you I drew the Southern Cross on our wedding cake," Grandma asked.

"That one you never told me."

"No one got it of course. It was our own private constellation wedding joke."

"Clever though. Two sailors plodding through life together."

"Now you're the cross Lenny."

"No I'm not."

"You didn't choose it," Grandma said.

"What are you saying Grandma?"

"I think you know."

* * *

Leisha and I drove to her house in complete silence.

"We shouldn't have been there," I finally said.

"I know, I know."

"I feel almost like we violated them," I said.

"I feel the same way."

Leisha was crying. No sobbing just silent tears running down her face.

"It all ends, doesn't it? We'll go out of each other's orbit, won't we?"

"We don't know that," I said.

"I wish they made a planisphere for relationships," Leisha said.

"I'm glad they don't."

FALL

It's hard to describe an Adirondack Fall if you haven't witnessed one.

Clichés are easy. Foliage ablaze with crimson and golden leaves. Abstract references to a beautiful tapestry of color. Summer on fire.

I won't try to give you those words. For me, it's not about describing the visual scene as much as it is about the other senses. The way it makes me feel.

In a word, I would say displacement. At peak, the scene is too intense to evaluate. It shuts one off. Shuts me down. I become removed from the world. No emails, no phone, no bills.

The same when you accidently remember the casual smile of a lost friend. When the shape of a cloud reminds you of a pet you loved. To be more mundane, a line from a Dead song you heard when you were seventeen, almost high, out of school, before work started.

So much world that it leaves you unworldly. Sensory overload, so powerful that it ironically removes you from the context that created it.

That first day Ronnie Jackson came back to town was such a day. I had popped a Bud and sat drinking it in the kid's old playhouse. I won't lie. I brought three more with me. I was finishing the second when Ronnie Jackson walked into my backyard. Hell, it had only been sixteen years.

"Partner," he said. "What the fuck you been up to?"

I took another sip of beer. "Ronnie Jack. In my fuckin' backyard. I'll be damned."

I stood up slowly and walked down the ramp that led up to the kitchen of the playhouse. Whether I should have or not, I extended my hand straight out to shake his. Patted him on the shoulder even. And yes, I noticed the trees, the colors, displacement ending.

"You got another Bud partner?"

"I can round one up I suppose."

I paused for a moment as the wind picked up. It still carried the warmth of summer, but not for long. There was an old poplar tree between the playhouse and the garage that was still mostly green. With the breeze lifting up and under the branches, it spun the green leaves in the sun like a thousand glittering monocles. I felt displacement again and to be frank, a sudden desire to get high.

"I'll grab you that beer Ronnie," I said, turning to the garage where I maintained a well stocked fridge.

The wind stopped as quickly as it had begun. When I walked by Ronnie toward the garage, he had the suggestion of a smirk on his face, but I let that go.

I grabbed two beers, ice cold, and we toasted.

"To old friends," Ronnie said.

"To old friends," I said, and added, "for sure."

Ronnie took a long drink of Bud and reached up to make a second toast.

"And to old secrets," he said.

In retrospect as I pounded the cold beer, so began a different kind of Adirondack fall.

* * *

16 Years Before

Margie Thompson was a good nurse having a very bad day. Any day at the Sunmount Developmental Center in Tupper Lake was a day offering challenges. Sunmount Developmental was such a professional and almost kind title for the centuries old complex of white washed brick buildings laying neatly on perfectly maintained grounds. Other than a small administrative building, the complex mainly housed hundreds of mentally ill patients in small, boxed rooms on halls laid out in the 1920s during the tuberculosis crisis.

At first glance, it could have been a college just outside of Tupper; classic architecture, the white brick softly blending with late autumn leaves. A closer look showed fencing and a secured entrance. No, it wasn't a college, it was an asylum on the edge of town.

Margie was working a double on a unit that was a nurse short already. The place reeked of institutional food mixed with old urine and intestinal gas. As she counted pills to distribute, near the nurses' station, ancient Waldon Johnson staggered down the hall. Not dangerous, not headed anywhere in particular, physically appearing well but in the final stages of Alzheimers. Nearby, in a corner, geriatric chair propped upright by a small stained pillow, sat Donald Lennox, just over eighty with the sad diagnoses of Palilalia, a word derived from the Latin for, again. The disease was now six decades old, a kind of a brain twitch that caused Donald to repeat the same words over and over again.

"As a matter of concern, Woodrow Wilson, Woodrow Wilson, this isn't new, Woodrow Wilson, Woodrow Wilson, yes I hear you mother, Woodrow Wilson, Woodrow Wilson, Woodrow Wilson."

Poor Donald had said the name Woodrow Wilson a thousand times each day for sixty years. The last time he said it, Margie looked up, saw the clock, 9:30 a.m.., looked back at the pills and realized she had lost count.

* * *

In a word, Ronnie Jack's accomplishments were effortless. He was an A student in all classes but excelled even beyond teacher expectations in science. He was a solid second baseman with a hitting record that exceeded 500 for every season in high school. His natural facial expression was a soft contracted jaw muscle that made him consistently appear to be both inhaling and smiling.

Oh, and he was the finest football quarterback in school history.

He was a running quarterback who could scramble out of traffic but just as easily relax in the pocket and throw darts downfield. By junior year, he had the attention of a dozen colleges. By senior year he had shattered our school's passing records and led the team in division victories against schools five times our size. In early November of 1980, he was on a tear like no one in our area had ever seen.

And, when it couldn't get any better, on a Tuesday morning in home-room, School Superintendent J. Richard Farrell could be heard clearing his throat over the school's decades old public address system to note: "I have an announcement of great importance for all students, faculty and administration. This morning via personal phone call from Congressman Richard Simms, I received confirmation that one of our own, Ronald Jackson, has been conditionally admitted to the U.S. Military Academy at West Point, Class of 1985."

Old man Farrell was a cold fish who never smiled. Never let his guard down and was blatantly opposed to the expression of personal emotions. So his next words were even more profound.

"On behalf of your entire school Ronnie Jack, you have done us proud."

In every room, K-12, spontaneous applause erupted. Even kids too young to understand what was happening, stood and clapped. Mr. Dakin, our chemistry teacher, discreetly wiped a tear from his eye.

And me, I was the dedicated side kick. I lumbered across home room, slapped Ronnie Jack on the back, feigned a quick Ali-Frasier boxing maneuver with him and said, "Not bad for a local."

Ronnie would head to officer's training and would try to walk on the Army football team. I was bound for state, less tuition, but I hadn't qualified for any scholarships.

I was Ronnie's tight end and working private protector on the field. I might catch a pass per game but my main job was blocking off the line and free lancing to give the QB added protection. He got the headlines and I was perfectly happy to float in his jet stream.

I also knew things that the others didn't know about Ronnie Jack. Both his parents were heavy drinkers, proud as hell, but unable to get out of their own way. They tried to be supportive but didn't know how. In some ways, he had become their parent. Knowing this that morning in home-room, it made Ronnie's on and off the field accomplishments even more impressive. Some nights after the big game, he wouldn't be out partying but rather, home being sure they got supper.

I also knew about the relationship with Kate. I knew it was important, more serious than most people suspected. She was two years older, already a sophomore at state. I think Ronnie wanted me there to be her protector the last two years as I had been his on the field. Twenty years old, seemingly mature with a flair for mischief. She was a brunette bombshell who was clearly spoken for.

Kate made it home for the big games. She stayed out of the spotlight, held his hand after the game but didn't kiss him in public. I knew what very few had figured out. Kate was his friend.

* * *

Visitors, even well meaning ones, added to the chaos. Timmy Larkin was being visited by his elderly parents who, in his delusional world, were trying to stab him. The phone rang on the nurse's station desk and Margie hoped someone would answer it or she would have to start counting meds all over again.

A nurse's aide finally picked up the phone on the eighth ring.

"Margie, it's your daughter calling from school. She's got the bug and needs to come home."

Margie went to the phone to talk directly to her daughter. There had been a number of false alarms since Ann had started junior high and she was going to have to tough it out and make the adjustment. Margie started confrontationally, which was a poor strategy.

"Ann, is this real, because I'm awfully busy."

"I just hurled in the girl's locker room so, yes, it is in fact real. I need to come home."

"I can't come get you for a few minutes at least."

Behind Margie there was a commotion. The Larkins had departed their son's room, Mrs. Larkin in tears. Timmy Larkin stood in the center of the hall and screamed, "Get them out of my room. They're not my parents. They're killers. I took a knife off the woman."

"Woodrow Wilson. And one more thing. Woodrow Wilson, Woodrow Wilson I'd say," muttered Donald Lennox.

Margie put the phone down and went to restrain Timmy Larkin. His parents turned, looked back once and then headed toward the exit at the end of the hall.

"In any regard, Woodrow Wilson."

"Timmy, come sit down with me," Margie said, in her best effort to stay calm. As she steered Timmy back to his room, the Larkins quietly walked out the door.

And just behind them, wearing a smart winter ski coat belonging to who knows who, the coat displaying a now out of style design called the wet look, strolled out Walden Johnson. He had to get something, something important but he couldn't remember what it was. But it was important. The fresh air felt good. He should get out more often, he thought, as he crossed Franklin Avenue.

* * *

It was a last minute decision. Ronnie Jack had found out Rory Broderick was going to work out with a D-3 college team in Canton, a couple hours north of town. Broderick was the only player in Upstate New York who was in Ronnie Jack's league. He was a rock solid quarterback we would face in just eight days in the league championship. Ronnie Jack was curious and a little bored at the end of 7th period study hall when he handed me a note that simply said, "road trip?"

Rory was good but not magical. When protection was sufficient he could usually deliver. When anything went wrong, he struggled to react. As Ronnie said, his mechanics were almost perfect when everything around him was good. But he lacked creativity. I remember Ronnie called Rory a "script QB." Stay on script, everything is great. Any deviation could mean trouble.

I met Rory three or four years later at a party. He was drunk and put his arm around me and said, "Shit man, I am so sorry about all that shit."

As we left we both agreed that next week would depend on how strong Rory's offensive line was and whether our defense could get him off script. As we drove out of Canton, Ronnie Jack said, "It's funny to think about next year, where we'll be at this time next year."

"It's pretty fucked up. You'll be in the Army. Dress gray. You should read that book before you go."

"I'm scared shitless about the whole thing. The Army, getting fucking hazed, and the academics are supposed to be brutal."

"No problem for the likes of Ronnie Jack, local hero."

"Yeah right. And you'll be at state. You going to try to play?"

"I've thought about it. I don't think so."

"And Kate's going to be a junior."

"Unbelievable."

"We're all fucking old."

* * *

Walden Johnson called the dog Maxine and enjoyed immensely scratching behind its scruffy ears. In 1951 Walden had purchased for his daughter Tammy, a small dog named Maxine and the family pet lived until Tammy had nearly finished college. He didn't remember that Maxine. In fact, he didn't remember Tammy, but he called the dog Maxine.

Because he had the ski jacket on, he had strolled right out of the facility. A guard likely assumed he was traveling with the Larkins.

Walden had placed a granola bar in his pants to have later after lunch last Tuesday. Maxine liked Walden, but loved the granola bar and so she started to follow him toward downtown Tupper Lake.

"Come on Maxine," Walden called.

The dog walked closer and pushed her nose into Walden's pocket.

There was a small coffee shop on a side street and Walden ordered a small coffee to go. He reached in his pocket and found the granola bar but no money. Where did he put his wallet?

"I'll be back to pay," Walden said as he stepped back outside the shop. Maxine had waited on the curb and her wait was rewarded. Walden pulled the wrapper off the granola bar and said, "Maxine, sit." Maxine did not sit. "Oh well," Walden said. "Maybe next time Maxine. You can have it any- ways." He handed the granola bar to Maxine.

In the distance he heard a police or fire siren blaring.

"It's always something isn't it old girl?'

* * *

As Maxine crunched on the granola bar and Walden stared down the street, Margie Thompson hung up the phone with the village police department and with great reluctance, pulled the emergency alarm at the nurse's station.

Maxine turned her head slightly. Something had spooked her. She jumped off the sidewalk directly into traffic. Walden yelled, "Maxine, get back here." And then he followed after her.

Maxine darted between a log truck and a passing school bus. She made her way across Main Street as Walden followed quickly along, trying not to lose visual contact. When he apprehended her on the opposite side of the road a police siren squealed even closer, turning into the service entrance of Sunmount.

It was the siren she hated. She bolted again. This time she scurried down a brick alleyway between the local hardware and Tupper Lake Baked Goods, pausing at the edge of Park Street. Walden approached and in the gentlest voice he could muster, being short of breath and feeling a pressure building in his chest and arms, said, "now Maxine, I might just have another treat."

Walden reached to pick her up, almost had her, when damn, more sirens. What kind of a town has a crime rate like this, he wondered. She jumped through his arms and bolted down Park Street, weaving between traffic moving in both directions. True to form Walden continued his pursuit.

Fortuitously, the traffic was letting up. In the distance, another log truck was approaching, having bypassed Main Street via Lake, to try to make up time. Maxine moved back to the sidewalk and downshifted to her cute little strut. Walden was four steps from her and would have her this time. In fact, she stopped as if to wait for him.

"That's my sweety," Walden whispered.

And for no reason whatsoever, Maxine wandered back into the road in time to be struck and crushed by the left fender of the log truck. She was thrown several yards and was killed instantly though she was still convulsing and shaking as Walden reached for her body.

He was overwhelmed by pain and sadness. It came from witnessing the accident and it seemed to pour from a multitude of sources he could not identify. The pain was strong enough to pass the long webbed synapsis and though its source, a wife, a mother, someone named Tammy, could not be remembered, the pain was real. The pain was overwhelming and extremely disorienting.

Carrying the warm corpse of Maxine against the ski parka, his institutional white pants now slightly soiled, Walden started down the center of Park Street as if he were beginning a pilgrimage. Had there been traffic, this scene would have surely stopped it. In the distance, a Chevy Citation turned off of Route 30 and onto Park. Perhaps the car was going a little fast. Perhaps there was a Molson Golden in the coffee holder. As the car approached, Walden, like Maxine before him, turned directly into traffic and was struck head on by the Chevy.

There was nothing left of Maxine. She had been struck twice in two minutes. Both Walden's thighs and pelvis were crushed on impact. His ribs fractured as he bounced up the hood and finally, directly on the windshield where the impact of the crash cracked the windshield, fractured his nose, his cheeks and freed several of his teeth, two of them lodging in the glass.

He was dead of course, eyes wide open, seeming simultaneously bewildered and in panic. He clutched what seemed like an unidentifiable mass of fur in his hands and stared straight at the two teenagers in the Chevy's front seat.

Inside the car, for what seemed like an hour, there was total silence. We were both in shock and mortified by the sight of an old man sprawled dead on the windshield.

In a moment, everything in our lives had changed. The log truck driver had never stopped after hitting the dog. Our accident had not been witnessed and there we sat in horrible silence. Ronnie began to cry hysterically. He would gather himself and then cry again. I began to cry too. The old man just stared at us.

In the quiet, after a few moments, Ronnie Jack turned to me and said, "Eddie, I'm fucked."

16 Years Later

I left Ronnie Jack drinking on the deck of the kids' playhouse to go inside for snack food. I moved over to my home office and began pilfering in the lower right drawer. I could see Ronnie through the side window and from a distance he looked alright. Tufts of sloppy hair moved in the breeze and as he turned his head, I noticed the half grin still intact. It was only close up to him that you noticed the pock marks in his skin, the long hair going prematurely white in several places. No doubt he needed money. There was no reason for him to be here. Even at this distance, he looked a little wired, agitated.

I pulled an old photo album from the bottom drawer and though it had been years, I found the press clipping tucked inside the cover, about how I left it more than a dozen years ago when we moved to a bigger house. I unfolded the clipping and read.

Allstar in Tupper Lake Fatality

Local sports star and high school senior, Ronald Jackson, was a passenger in a car involved in a traffic fatality here yesterday, leaving dead a resident of the Sunmount Facility.

At press time, it was unclear why the resident was off facility grounds but it is believed he had wandered to Park Street in the Village. The victim's name is being withheld at this time. Jackson, a four sport all star and quarterback of the Tupper Lake High School team, scheduled to compete in a state championship game next week, was not charged.

The driver of the vehicle, Edward Densmore, was charged with reckless driving, arraigned and released on $5000 bail from Tupper Lake Village Court. Law Enforcement sources confirmed that more serious charges could be forthcoming.

Densmore is a high school senior and a member of the football team as well.

Jackson was believed to be the only other passenger in the vehicle, which struck and killed the pedestrian and is not expected to face charges of any sort.

Jackson had recently announced his intention to attend the U.S. Military Academy at West Point in the fall.

Neither Jackson nor Densmore were injured in the crash. An investigation is ongoing.

I was immediately suspended from school and of course the football team. I sat in a low row of bleachers the afternoon of the championship in jeans and an old sweatshirt. I was apparently toxic as no member of the team even spoke to me. Several times I would see a parent pointing me out to another stunned adult, who would shake his head and turn away.

Rory Brockerick didn't have an offensive line, he had an immoveable, impenetrable wall protecting him. We were outsized and outrun in almost every position, thus permitting Rory to stay fully on script. In the first half, he went eighteen of twenty- one in passing and threw for two touchdowns.

Ronnie Jack tried to make something happen with little success. He never had enough protection and as the game progressed into the 4th quarter, his own line was exhausted. The defensive line began to sack him at will. Fourth and three, down seventeen, with four minutes left, the coach waved the offense back onto the field. What else could he do?

The play called for Ronnie to roll right. He had the option of pitching right to a back or looking for a wide out in the middle. He stepped back into shot gun formation, called for the snap and as it hit his hands he briefly disconnected and shut down. He bobbled the ball, then dropped it. The line couldn't hold and a moment later Ronnie was buried beneath a pile of six players. He pulled his helmet off and limped across the field.

* * *

I threw a bag of unopened Doritos in Ronnie Jack's general direction.

"Help yourself," I said.

"Look at you Eddie. You sure did alright. This house is beautiful, kids, the wife. You must make a pretty penny off of your insurance business."

"I also work my ass off. I'm in most Saturdays. I bid on nearly every school district and town within 150 miles."

"Looks like it pays off," Ronnie said.

"We're comfortable. We'll definitely have too big a house when both girls are in college."

"Not a bad problem to have Eddie."

"I guess not. What about you Ronnie? How have you been?"

"I do alright. In a tight spot right now, but I'll get by. I always seem to."

I paused for a moment and then surprised myself. Turning the conversation in a direction I never thought I would go.

"What the fuck ever happened to you and West Point. Do you know the rumors floating around this town back then?"

"I imagine. I can sure imagine. Especially when I never came back home."

"Next time I saw you was at your mother's funeral but that was, God, at least a couple of years later."

"They got this thing there, when you leave after just two years. They call it turn left. Well my parents couldn't drive me out there and I hitched a ride with another kid's family. We got dropped in the lot. They said their goodbyes and I wandered over to the sidewalk where everyone was walking in. I got talking to another kid. He was freaking out a little."

"About West Point?"

"Oh yeah, there's a lot to freak out about. He told me he'd heard they tried to drown the Plebes in the swimming pool. Told me the first year was condensed hell. They call it Beat Barrack. He was scared. I think I actually reassured him a bit. A minute later he slung his bag over his shoulder and headed down the walkway to be processed and shaved."

"And Ronnie Jack?"

"Seems like Ronnie Jack didn't step left. I simply turned straight around."

"You didn't even walk in?"

"Never wanted a beer so bad in my life. Turned around and started walking out. I couldn't see myself there any longer. I didn't fit."

"Jesus Ronnie."

"Hey, no regrets buddy, no regrets."

"I guess not."

"The beer was good. Found a taproom in Highland Falls. Billy Joel used to drink at the same place. And no shit, I proceeded to tie one on."

"I bet."

"Got my ass arrested for public indecency. I guess I took a piss on the town hall. I have no recollection of it."

"And then what happened?"

"Kate's parents found me. Posted bail. It was bad shit. They wanted me to go to rehab. You probably know the rest of it."

"Why the hell didn't you go back to college?"

"I tried a couple of times. It didn't take. Almost walked on to a semi pro team in Albany but that's when my knee started to swell. Look, I'm all for memory lane partner, but I'm in a jam. If I had some where's else to go I would have."

"How much Ronnie?"

After a long pause, the glued on half smile now looking more like a facial tick, sweat covering his forehead, Ronnie said, "Eddie, I need $7500 or I might be a dead man."

"Jesus Christ Ronnie."

It became business after that. I cut Ronnie a check and we quickly shook hands. I watched him back out of the driveway and pull away. Most of the light had gone out of the day. I started to pick up the garage and tossed the empties. He'd never opened the chips. Gradually I began to feel I was being observed. I looked towards the road and of course saw absolutely nothing. I turned around near the back of the garage where some old storm windows had been in storage for years. As I looked at the glass I realized just who had been watching me. Face contorted, bewildered, one eye now bleeding, staring straight into my eyes was Walden Johnson. I had never been able to remember his face. Since the day of the accident .it had bothered me. The photo in his obituary had been taken when he was a young man, maybe just thirty. We were locked together for just a few moments time. He already passed and me on the front edge of disaster.

I looked away, blinked a tear out of my eye and turned back to the storm. I whispered to myself, "this probably needed to happen."

I got back to business. Finished cleaning up and turned the outside lights on for the girls. They were due within an hour and their mother most any minute.

I folded the article back up and thought about throwing it away but I didn't. I turned the TV on. NFL Sunday. Everyone would assume it was another Sunday of sports and someone would make a joke about a man cave. I saw headlights turn into and up the driveway. Ronnie Jackson had his money but I'm sure that wouldn't end his problems. I was glad that I had at least turned him around before Kate got home.

HIGH CRIMES
& GEWURZTRAMINERS

In fairness, being the Fuhrer's granddaughter has cramped my lifestyle very little until recently. I know your first thought, perhaps sitting in your overstuffed Stickley armchair on your cookie cutter cul-de-sac, the mad man left no progeny. You have Uncle Steve, a dentist from Farmingdale who passed away in his sleep and Granny Whistlethinner, who gave her life to the church after Pappy mounted the dry cleaner's wife. And I have the wax figure under glass at Madame Tussauds, drugged up and taking the other woman with him as the Russians moved toward the Chancellery.

Your first thought is text book and quite wrong. To be sure, there is no suggestion of me or my mother anywhere. Our past is a secret, one I can't believe I write of here. My maternal grandmother was Geli Rabaul, the one you might have read of, offing herself after the relationship went south. But wait, there's more. There was a baby, a secret little bundle of Nordic joy, a true Hitler youth, raised quietly in the countryside, told nothing until the age of thirty when secrets have significance, my mother.

Did he know? We know not. My mother was told by an aunt in 1960. I speculate sometimes at the delivery of the thing. "Oh, by the way, your father killed six Million Jews." Or maybe, "Daddy conquered the world, but he was a little eccentric." Or possibly, "Papa Adolph was one wild and crazy guy."

Occasionally, I'll be standing in front of my 10th grade literature class and I will feel the excitement about some great work of art. I'm pumped, passionate and the words roll from my mouth, "Of course, Gatsby never reached the green light near the end of Daisy's pier, the past receding out of reach. It's why home was only what we imagined it to be. It exists as an invention of our brain."

I'm perspiring now and some students might say, "Ms. Doyle was on a roll today." The words are out of me before I think of them. They are still hot, glowing coals as they hit the minds of post pubescent adolescents struggling with erections and lunch hunger and the death of some distant rap star a million miles away from this tiny district where my great-aunt summered us from NYC because she concluded that the Adirondacks were the American version of the Black Forest. And I feel in the groove, flowing, reaching them and suddenly, abruptly, the bell rings and only by an act of will can I stop the lecture and acknowledge in my own mind, my secret world. The talking is my Grandfather's gift, a knotty jumble of blood and DNA. I'm an orator, be it 10th grade English or the Nuremburg Rally. I'm a Hitler.

* * *

He was wearing a tattered Derek Jeter t shirt and had an ipod plugged into his ear. He'd probably smoked a joint at lunch hour, although he wasn't too much into pot during ball season. He was never a stellar student, devoting his time mostly to varsity basketball and the girl du jour. For some reason, that day though, he was under my skin more than normal and I must have shown my frustration.

To clarify somewhat, he wasn't failing the class, just doing enough to survive. His parents had money and he was thought to be hot by the seventeen year old crowd, although I didn't see it.

What sort of man is the public school English teacher, granddaughter of the world's most demonic dictator, attracted to? More normal than you'd think. No, I don't need to be in control nor have I for one minute understood bondage. I read the book that said my Grandfather liked to be defecated on and pardon the pun, but I'm not into that shit.

I guess I like a man that I'll never be with. A man like Tom Littman, whom I dated quietly for almost three years. He taught math at a neighboring school and took night classes in public administration. We might sit together and never talk. We were comfortable together. I loved the way he tended his summer garden with great attention to the order in each row and a grand commitment to the tedium of weeding. He treated me well enough but never doted. I could maneuver my life about as I liked and our relationship was the constant, unobtrusive yet available.

As I stood looking at Derek Jeter, I thought of how being with Tom had been like my teenage summers in the Adirondacks with my mother and great aunt. Board games and cards. Much ado about backgammon and campfires. A lot of activity and not much analysis. I think the reason I got so ripped at Derek Jeter at that moment was because I remembered losing Tom as the school year began. Losing him because one night in late August, I'd put away the backgammon game and told him my secret. He was the only one I ever told and I did so in clinical terms because I was unsure what to expect of myself.

"I am forty years old. I am a high school English teacher. I am single, never married. I have brown eyes, dark features, dark hair that curls around itself as it flows down my neckline. I'm a decent skier and love to swim. My father, John Doyle, was a tax attorney who died of a myocardial infarction when I was six years old. I began traveling to the Adirondacks with my mother and great aunt when I was a little girl. My great aunt said the mountains reminded her of the Fatherland. My mother's maiden name was Robal, but her birth certificate reads Raubal. My mother was the daughter of Geli Raubal and her great love, Adolph Hitler."

There, I thought, I've said it. I've said it to another person. There was an instant of silence and the slightest suggestion of a smile before Tom replied, "And I'm the son of Ferdinand Marcos."

The anger was not just in the relationship ending once Tom believed me, but also the acknowledgment that all future relationships ended with it. I knew I'd never get this far with a man again, probably never try. A week later, Tom told me he couldn't reconcile himself to it. His grandfather's brother had been killed at Bergen-Belsen. "I didn't do it," I pleaded. "It happened thirty years before I was born."

"I know, I know," he said. "Look.," he added. "I promise to never tell. Never a word."

So, I was preoccupied, off my game, when I ripped into Derek Jeter. And the timing was horrendous also. I was just a few weeks away from tenure review and here I was, losing it with a student.

As Derek Jeter walked out of class that day, he scowled at me and brushed his hip against my desk, pushing it into me.

"You oughta chill, you fucking Nazi," Derek Jeter said.

* * *

Let's start with candor. If I'm to finish this accounting, I must pledge honesty. I must come clean on many of the seemingly minor transgressions that marked the roadway to calamity. Call it this, "Chapter the Third, I move to Hard Liquor." Specifically, vodka, ice cold, beaded Stoli from freezer to glass and closing now with Beaujolais to bring fast, hard, forgetful sleep. There you have it, Russian vodka, French table wine and another Hitler losing a two front war.

It was never about the pilates, my thrice weekly journey to a small gym some thirty miles away. True enough, I liked the words, *finding balance, inner core muscles and full body and mind toning.* I bought a duffel bag too and folded quite neatly my new stretch bands and workout wear with a thick towel.

They had just announced on the car radio it was the anniversary of Columbine and I'm drawn to that memory. It was, of course, before Tom Littman, before the new school and before I knew I would be seeking a new job. Mother was alive and we watched it together on the kitchen TV while seated at the table. And we watched days later, as the story evolved. A trench coat duo of social outcasts intent on revenge against the cliques in a well to do public school. Shoot the jocks, shoot the babes with nice tits, shoot the coaches and the starters on the varsity football team. And of course, all inspired by none other than my Grandfather.

I saw her sink into the chair. Felt her shutting down, moving on now, getting by it in her own way.

"You, Lisa, put the casserole in the oven and I'll pull some beans from the garden," she said.

I saw her stooped outside the window in her old housedress, meticulous as always, picking green beans, nabbing only the plumpest from each plant, discarding the weaker ones that threatened the growth of the strong. I glanced quickly into the casserole dish as I slid it over the oven rack. And there, amidst the bubbling pasta and cheese, carefully spiced from an old family recipe, I saw them, faces.

Not about pilates then, but staggered liquor purchases in another town. Three nights a week I run no risk of buying vodka in front of a school board member or my wine while someone from the tenure peer committee looks on. *Hello Ms. Doyle. It seems I see you here too often,* they might say.

That night I bought more vodka and reverted to white wine, because it was hot, humid, a suggestion of the summer to come. I put a towel around my neck to make the clerk think I was coming from a workout, and made my buy. I got back in my car, no, not a Volkswagen or something from the Bavarian Motor Works, I won't buy Toyota or Nissan because of ToJo. I read that Ford was an anti-semite. I drive a Chevy.

Ten minutes from home, the dense humidity gave way to a spray of rain. The creeks and rivers began to swell, the road became dark and slick. I let off the accelerator, down shifted and was tempted, knowing the white wine was a twist off. Up ahead was a lumber mill that must have employed half the town, but closed at this hour. Walking near the mill property, elbows contorted and using the varsity letter jacket as a cover for his head, was Derek Jeter.

* * *

I am seated at the end of a long table at one of the school's administrative offices, ankles crossed, my hands clasped before me. I chose the navy blue suit because it was safe and conservative. I am wearing a brooch with a tiny photo of my great aunt secreted inside. This is only social conversation. I am a good teacher. I will be tenured. It is assured.

Ida Milt is there. The dear school librarian, six months shy of retirement. Tom Daniels, junior high chemistry teacher who wants to be done with all this in time to catch the Red Sox game, and of course, Tom Littman, representing school administration, recently promoted and reassigned to my district. They will review my regents pass rates, touch on my personnel file and my extra curricular activity. I am ok. And I remind myself, I am human. By definition, weak and vulnerable to mistakes. And this had been a big one.

* * *

We drank the wine from the bottle as we drove towards town. The rain became thunderous, the wipers barely able to keep pace as sheets of water pounded the windshield.

"Pull over a minute," he said. "This isn't safe." And I did.

I had offered him a ride and pulled over when he told me to. I let him twist the cap off the wine, hearing each click of the metal breaking free on the bottle neck as distinct as gunfire. I let him drink the wine. I let him hand it back to me. I held the bottle to my mouth, felt the beads of condensation around the small glass, saw a mark where his mouth had been. Every action a decision. Even inaction a decision as well. I drank with him.

A moment later I felt the coolness of the wine burning its path from esophagus to stomach. And he drank again. I said to him, "Did you ever think you'd drink with a Nazi?" And we laughed. I felt his hard on against my thigh and chose not to stop it, at least not yet. A powerful hand sliding upward, up and under my skirt. Not stopping him yet, deciding, tasting the wine in his mouth. The hand higher, spinning as the rain carved deep gullies in the sand to carry the runoff downhill and away from the American made car, where Hitler's granddaughter was making it with one of her students a week before peer review.

It was Tom Littman's voice that brought me back.

"Do you have any questions for the committee about the balance of the process or the time frame, or anything else you can think of?"

Recovering, reorienting, I responded professionally. "No, I think I've developed an understanding of the process."

"Very good. We are done and I will provide you a final opportunity to address the review committee." He shifted his chair. This part was unscripted. Somehow, I knew what was coming.

"Is there any disclosure you wish to make to the committee that might impact our review process or reflect upon the school, should you receive an award of tenure? Anything we need to know about you or your history?"

There he was, on the moral high ground. His balance achieved by dumping it in my lap to decide. He can say to himself, "look, I gave her the opportunity to tell us, and she made a choice." He could likewise feel he had protected me by not forcing the admission as to my ancestry.

I paused before answering him and excused myself from the room.

* * *

The New York State Teacher's Union is among the most powerful labor organizations on the planet. The body rules public education with an unbreakable force of blood and iron. Today's teacher is the public sector benefactor of five thousand labor disputes fought by union forces over the decades. Limitless payrolls fund the best attorneys, the strongest lobbyists and the best candidates. And what successes have been achieved? Twenty year state retirement with health care, fourteen months pay for nine months works and of course the holy grail, tenure.

109

Tenure, my teacher's union handbook explains, is about owning your future. More than just job security, tenure in the public schools constitutes a property interest in one's career. For all intents and purposes, tenured teachers can't be fired. Once tenured, the union has your back, and are prepared to fight even unworthy causes, to the death. Post tenure teachers don't worry much. Historically intended to protect academic freedom, the concept has mutated into something quite different in public school; the freedom to teach badly or not teach at all. Tenure eliminates consequences for conduct, standing any sort of merit system on its head. It's like a public school contraceptive, fuck around all you want, you can't get pregnant or fired.

Fraulein Lisa Doyle is on track for tenure in my fourth year teaching in this tiny district. All is in order with little to worry about. I view myself as an exception to those notions of lazy teachers in sweater vests, counting the days until investiture in the state retirement system. I love my job and love to teach. I've always loved my books, and no, I've never read his. I tried once, quietly and secretly, in the back bedroom of my apartment, with just one light on and a blanket pulled to my neck as if I were masturbating or sneaking a joint. My grandfather could do many things, but Mein Kampf proved to a certainty that he couldn't write worth a shit.

I put the book down after several pages of trying to sort though his crazy plan to find living space for pure Germans in the lands vacated by the murdered Slavic races. I turned all the lights on and ran water from all the taps. I found myself wheezing a bit when I removed the tiny, tightly bound book from my living room shelves and began reading. The Diary of Anne Frank, my act of contrition like the monks who flog themselves for thinking about corsets.

Tenure was an opportunity to control my future, to establish a steady, protected path toward retirement. Like everyone, I want what's best for myself. I want a hand in controlling my future, but I have no say over my past. There is no tenure for genealogy.

And then I said aloud, to no one at all, "but there's chilled white wine in the fridge." And somewhere between the little girl who died seeing the good in all people and the psychopathic God, I drank the entire bottle.

I was mad to do what I did. I concede that now. Standing at a distance, I know that it was wrong, yes, but not premeditated. It began as a slippery slope, the warning signs were not just unheeded, but unseen.

It began the day Derek Jeter stayed after school to speak with me. I coach junior varsity field hockey, and was in a rush, with no need for another confrontation with the school jock.

"Ms. Doyle," he said.

"What is it? I'm late for practice."

To my surprise, he apologized.

"I wanted to tell you I'm sorry."

"You're sorry," I questioned him.

"For calling you a Nazi," he explained. "You see we just started a unit on the Holocaust in social studies, and well, I was pretty pissed off but I shouldn't have called you a Nazi. I didn't understand how those people were capable of that crazy shit."

I was taken aback but thanked him as I grabbed the laptop where I kept grades, a folder of tenth grade essays on Arthur Miller's The Crucible and trotted to the sanctuary of the girls' squad. This was a few days before the car but I had felt something and was very confused.

That night I called Tom Littman. I really had no one else. Mother died of brain cancer before I was offered the new teaching job. My friends were social contacts at best. There was no one ready to deal with the feeling that somewhere inside myself was a blood line, a contamination both abhorrent and strangely prideful, a capacity for atrocity.

It wasn't wrong to call Tom. We had agreed to talk, to stay friends. He even said once, "who knows…" Tom was on staff at my school now. He had finished his doctoral work and had been appointed elementary principal. I saw more of him. He was always positive and friendly, with never a suggestion of my secret, or even our past relationship. It felt like we were pretending we could start over.

I was wrong to drink the Reisling or the Gewurztraminer or whatever it was. It made me cry with Tom and never tell him why. I didn't tell him about Derek Jeter or the Holocaust unit or even Arthur Miller. I just cried without telling him why and woke in the morning feeling like a bomb had squarely hit the Fuhrer's bunker.

* * *

The week before spring recess, I received notice of my successful peer review. It was part one of the tenure process with nothing unexpected. I remember holding the document in my hand, standing next to my mailbox, "Ms. Doyle, High School English," and feeling a mixture of surrealism and grogginess. I'd had a disturbing dream the night before, and even with coffee and Advil, I couldn't shake it off.

In my dream, Lenny Riefenstahl had been hired to film a documentary about the school. This was not the daring and dashing Lenny of the 1930s and 1940s, but rather the old recluse granting rare interviews to deny the Nazification of her art. She had climbed some scaffolding in the gym where boys' basketball practice was underway as she tried to shout through an old style producers cone.

"Don't shoot layups! No one wants to see a film about layups. Jump shots please, top of the key."

Turning to the side, she cried out, "Where are the cheerleaders? There must be young, round, panty wrapped asses for the final scene." Then "aww, Fraulein Doyle, climb the scaffold and greet me."

I started to climb as she filmed the jump shots and lined up the cheerleaders, each with a letter glued to the backside of her panties. Without the proper order, nothing would come of it.

I climbed higher and higher, shimmying my way from pipe to pipe, foothold to foothold, until finally, I crested the top of the scaffold where Lenny and the cameraman presided over the controlled chaos below.

"My God. My God, girl. The eyes. You have his eyes."

"What's the movie about?"

"It's something between Porky's III and Sophie's Choice."

"Will there be real actors or just the school children?"

"It makes no difference."

Suddenly, the cameraman shouted, "Lenny, Lenny, the girls, they are lined up now."

Lenny shouted down to them, "now bend over ladies! Nordic asses in the air."

It was only a dress rehearsal and some letters were out of order. "Letter U, trade places with Letter E. That's good. That's it. Now you have it."

And from my perch atop the filmmakers' scaffold, I squinted to make out the words spelled on the cheerleaders' asses:

TENURE

* * *

Tom Littman had surprised me with a kind note of congratulations
and a bottle of Cabernet. For some reason, I did everything I could to avoid
him. It was the last question in peer review. Tom, in his soft, professional
delivery, asking for an accounting of my history and forcing me to make
the decision of denial. Denial of what he knew and of course, denial of
what he did not. Sins that I was born to and sins that I created.

There was a quiet pull off on the Eastern side of the Hudson River
just above North Creek. Sometimes I walk there to try to clear my head,
or as I heard from another teacher recently "to press reset." The river is
shallow, with only a few good swimming spots. Upriver, to the North, is
Sullivan's Island, the river separating around it and then rejoining.

Across the river are the remains of old garnet sheds and a few teens
are swimming there, drinking beer and laughing. Who can blame them?
Today was the last regents exam for the senior class. They're entitled. Let
them have their moment.

Looking downriver is the tiny hamlet. An old wood mill, the famous
train station and the old Waddell Store complex. Once you could buy coal
there, or grain. Even a stagecoach ticket. This afternoon it is the staging
area for the first farmer's market of the season, one of the only venues
where locals and tourists co-exist.

I am looking at the river but thinking about what is behind me. I am
technically on her land when I am at this part of the river. It's a pine shin-
gled house, painted brown and sitting squarely in the middle of a massive
field. Her husband had gardened this field extensively, but he had been
gone five years now. The former gardens gave way to tall grass that moved
noticeably in a light breeze. I turn away from the river and look toward the
house. Ellen is in there right now, I think. A ninety four year old invalid

with around the clock care. A gracious lady I had met several times when my mother was still alive. There are no children, no grand kids to run across the sweeping field or play in the rock outcropping behind the main house.

She had wanted nothing but a large family in this safe country place, but Mengele and his henchmen had destroyed her ovaries in the birth control experiments. Mengele, who worked for my Grandfather, Ellen, who befriended my mother. Tom Littman, my love that I cannot love. Derek Jeter, whom I didn't love, but had willingly lusted after.

I read the grant of tenure letter one more time. It was security for me. It couldn't be taken away. I folded it, stuffed it in my pocket, and once again stared at Ellen's house. A property interest in my career. But what do you really own? What can you really change? I imagine Ellen in there now, struggling to work one of her beloved crafts. Her arthritic hands have likely made her hobbies nearly impossible.

I turn away from the house and try for a moment not to think of her. I do something I have never done on these recent walks. I slip my shoes off, roll my pants up above my knees and ever so carefully, wade into the river.

INTERSECTION

The war protester's name was Ivan Berdosky. He was in his mid- fifties, heavy, in a long green coat and a beard that hadn't been trimmed since Iran Contra. He stood alone at the four corners of the small hamlet as he had every Friday at 4 p.m. since the bombing had begun. He carried a sign around his neck that said, "Honk for Peace."

Not many people honked. A veteran supply officer from the Korean conflict drove by each Friday at 4:30 and gave him the finger. He was once mooned by a ninth grader on the girl's field hockey team, a highlight really. Bed, peace. All in the kaleidoscope of protest memories. A few friends waved, or called out, "give' em hell Ivan.:" But not many honked.

The third Friday a photographer from the paper in Glens Falls traveled north in a GMC Jimmy and took his picture. Ivan had been eating, was chewing jelly beans when the picture was snapped. The next morning on A1, he look deranged, beard blowing in the autumn wind, mouth snarled, but Ivan knew it was only the jelly beans.

In late September a tourist from Manhattan slowed, looked at Ivan and with unmistakable clarity, honked. The next Friday Ivan had the same sign on his front, but across his back, bouncing awkwardly off the butt of his old carpenter's jeans was the new sign. The new sign said "Honk if you've seen a weapon of mass destruction." Ivan stood on the corner for three hours, both signs visible. No one honked. In ambiguity, he had found victory. No one honked.

At the end of September, something truly amazing happened. Something Ivan wasn't prepared for. A local woman in a Ford 4 by 4 slowed, honked, rolled down her window and called out, "What in the hell we doing there anyway Ivan?"

The first Friday of October Ivan arrived with still another sign. This one said, "Make Peace, Eat Bush." At 6:30 p.m. a sheriff's deputy arrived, called dispatch for counsel and left without making an arrest.

Leroy Baker, President Emeritus of the VFW, had had enough. The next Friday, he and ten veterans in tightly pressed uniforms, blue legion caps and perfect black shoes, appeared across the street from Ivan, each carrying a sign that read, "United We Stand."

None of the VFW signs said honk, but still many people did. A man who worked for the local highway department paused in front of Ivan, rolled down his window and called out, "Ivan, you're fucked."

Ivan was elated.

* * *

Many years before, Ivan worked on Long Island as a diesel mechanic. He had moved to the Adirondacks only after a work site injury had forced him out of the union, but provided a regular disability check. When Ivan and Loretta moved to North Creek, only their youngest daughter, Dorothy, was still in school. She was in the 9th grade. Ivan had named her Dorothy because of the world she was born into, but it hadn't stuck. Everyone on the Island and later in the mountains called her Dortie. This was ten years ago, Dortie was now a mother of her own with a home based hemp business. Back then though, Dortie was baggie jeans, sweatshirts with no bras and listening to music called grunge, which most people were already over.

Dortie wasn't popular, or unpopular. She was just sort of there. Oddly, she sometimes wore an army combat shirt with sergeant's stripes. Nobody knew where it came from, Dortie wasn't saying.

All through high school, Dortie was Dortie, unkempt, attractive in a primitive way, ganja supplier to the class of 2004, doing nothing out of character. Nothing at all, except for once.

It happened in November of her senior year. After school, on a blustery rain soaked day, when the school gym seemed a warm reprieve from the outdoors. That day Dortie, nicely showered, pits shaved, smelling mildly of wildflowers, emerged from the girl's locker room and in tight shorts, sports bra and with ribbons in her hair, tried out for and made the varsity basketball cheerleading squad.

Ivan was perplexed but proud. It was exactly as he had said so many years ago, the world she was born into.

She was a good cheerleader too. Not the lead, but steady, solid on splits, high jumps, nicely pitched voice. Midway into the season, she had even invented a cheer, one that Coach Bertry thought was clever, appropriate. She called it "Smells Like Team Spirit."

Sometimes, before games or more likely at half time, she and another cheerleader, Tonda Hall, would share a joint in the car her father had bought for her at Christmastime, using the proceeds of the final payment in his worker's compensation suit. The car was a Neon, made in Detroit, but the grass was usually Hawaiian, powerful and sublime.

One night, Dortie and Tonda came back totally stoned, laughing at each other through the second half like they were sharing a private joke. They were of course, since no one suspected a thing. That night Johnsburg was playing Lake George and playing very well. The game was like a vortex to Dortie. She did her cheers, smiled robotically, but for once just reveled in watching the game. The forward, Jeremy Dorr, was on fire. He had played a solid first half, but in the third quarter was unstoppable. He hit two jump shots from the perimeter and moments later, his sweating bangs slopping from left to right, drove to the hoop for a three- point play. In the 4th quarter with only a minute left, Jeremy stole the ball from a Lake George guard, drove full court and sunk a layup. The layup marked his thirty eighth and thirty ninth points. The next day the newspaper would call Jeremy's performance "top notch, noteworthy, inspiring." But for Dortie and Tonda, the ganja girls of the varsity squad, the real memory of that game, their last, came a few minutes later when Mrs. Bertry freed them of their pom poms, saying succinctly, "my girls don't smoke dope."

* * *

One Friday, near the end of October, a ruckus erupted between Ivan and the vets. It was just like Lexington and Concord, afterwards no one was truly sure who fired the first shot. By the end of it though, one of the vets had hurled a soda can at Ivan and Ivan had coarsely suggested that the vet might do better screwing little Cambodian girls.

The next Friday, there were a dozen more vets in pressed uniforms, well behaved and carrying larger signs. The same day Ivan showed up alone as always, but was emotionally overwhelmed when Dortie and her boyfriend Russell showed up with peace signs of their own.

There were no more confrontations between the two sides. In fact, after some days on the line, a mutual respect emerged. When the signs were folded into trucks and SUVs, Ivan would walk across the road and shout, "See you next Friday Leroy." Leroy would call back, "Have a good weekend Ivan, keep your ass out of trouble."

* * *

In high school, Tonda Hall was not a slut. Nor was she struggling to free her maidenhood from the constraints of Victorian repression. She felt pretty much like Dortie did, sex was ok but more often than not it screwed things up more than it was ever worth.

Tonda had gone out with a few guys, a guy she had dropped acid with from another school, the bass player for a loud, oldies band and mainly a friend of her brothers who visited mostly on weekends from Poughkeepsie.

As a ganja girl she was simply not the type for the likes of Jeremy Dorr. Certainly, she was gorgeous without trying, usually wearing tight jeans that belled at the ankle and a skin tight pull over top. Her coal black hair was simply rubber banded behind her head, her cheeks round and high, looking like maybe a runway model who'd slept three nights in the same clothes and couldn't be bothered.

The thing with Jeremy started a week after Mrs. Bertry bounced the girls from the squad. Tonda and Dortie dressed to the nines and showed up for the next game, their two cheering slots filled by a couple of peppy sophomores brought up from JV. They decided not to get high at half time since Bertry would patrol the parking lot like a mad trooper. After the game though, they drove in the Neon to a post game party, just outside of town, along the Hudson River. By the time they got there a bonfire was already torched and a few cases of beer were being shared by ball players and other kids from the school.

As it got colder, everyone moved in closer around the fire, huddled together, most drinking, some smoking cigarettes. Jeremy was drinking a Budweiser and wearing his varsity jacket and a Boston Celtics baseball cap. He'd scored twenty points against Hartford that night with a half dozen assists. When someone handed him a joint, he passed it on, not really interested. Mr. Clean, Tonda thought, big jock. Wally Rogers, a younger kid, was in the Neon with Dortie, no doubt doing bong hits or something and Tonda was standing by the fire. This wasn't her crowd, but when she looked back and saw the light go off in the Neon, she knew she'd hang by the fire.

That's when she started talking to Jeremy Dorr. Later, she'd have no idea what they'd talked about, just casual, but he was easy to talk to. He drove her home in his father's truck, a good twenty minute drive out past Garnet Lake and down a dirt driveway to the cabin Tonda's mother had moved to after her father had bailed. They had only one cigarette between them and made a deal to share it. He left the truck off and a window open for the smoke and soon enough it was cold as hell. She leaned into him, mainly to stay warm and he handed her back the cigarette and put his arm around her. It wasn't in a big brother way, but it wasn't in a gay way either. It was confidential. It was sublime. It reminded her of the maui wowie.

* * *

Ivan was famous for being a war protester but it wasn't all he did. Tuesdays and Thursdays he drove Loretta to dialysis in Albany and with her frailty had grown to be a fine cook in his own right. On most Fridays he would stir fry vegetables in a large wok he had purchased at a second hand shop in Troy, add tofu and soy sauce. He would wheel Loretta to the table and dish out food for her and sometimes Russell and Dortie. There was no TV in the house but he had an old record player and most nights during dinner the crackling sound of the Velvet Underground served as a back drop for an all organic feast. Loretta's appetite was never the best after treatment and the long drive home, but she always raved about some part of each night's dinner and Ivan would smile proudly.

After Dortie and Russell started joining in the Friday war protests, they made it a point to return for a family dinner with Ivan and Loretta. Some Fridays Dortie brought her special lemon meringue pie as a treat. Once, without announcement, she had prepared a double chocolate layer cake laced with hash and even Loretta had eaten a second piece.

On a Friday in early May, after three hours on the street corner, she and Russell arrived to find Loretta asleep in her wheelchair, facing out the old storm window, eyes closed as a snow flurry danced in front of her drooped head. They let her sleep through dinner and later, Dortie holding Russell's long stringy finger with one hand and nervously playing with her beads with the other, announced what Ivan had long suspected. She was carrying Russell's love child. The child, a boy, was born just six months after high school graduation, at home in the bathtub with Russell and Ivan both coaching as the baby boy emerged from the womb and surfaced in the warm, bloody water of the tub.

Ivan held the screaming infant in his hands, wide grin spread across his face.

"Well Dortie, he's a squawker, what are you going to name him?"

Dortie was exhausted, still lying in the tub and apparently in a state of semi consciousness.

"Cobain Daddy, has to but one name for my little boy. Cobain."

* * *

It took Tonda a long time to understand what she really liked about Jeremy, but eventually it came down to two different things. In the weeks after the party, he had driven her home a few times, sat with her in study hall and had dinner once with her mother. They talked constantly and smoked cigarettes all the time. All the while though, he seemed to learn about her, her parents divorce, what it felt like to be totally stoned, her friends, but he gave up little. Talked about basketball. He like to pass more than shoot, about his little brother, about him wanting to fly or work on planes. But in the end, she felt revealed to him and he seemed distant, just out of reach, not like a tough guy, but a sweet guy encapsulated. She liked it. It was a challenge to get to him, it made her smile when she sensed him change gears in mid sentence to give up saying something with real meaning. He was self protective and so she let go even more. Old boyfriends, her father, the friendship with Dortie. He kept within strict lines of protocol and she knew no bounds. It turned her on.

The other thing she liked, and it took her even longer to understand this, was his ambition. It wasn't just the planes, it was a vibe he gave off like an aura, like what he wanted, was about to happen, was a matter of more work, more practice, patience. Inevitable success slowly unrolling. Take your time. Hurry up.

It worked because they had become fast friends first and lovers much later. It also worked because she trusted him, something previously reserved for Dortie only.

And of course, it made for problems with Dortie too. Dortie still expected a hit on the way to school, Tonda in the Neon on the way home, listening to a summary of some Saturday night's events. But it had changed and Dortie resented it. Resented how odd they looked together, the stoic clean cut jock and the defrocked model, former pot head. Later, she was angrier still because after the initial shock, they looked right together. They fit. It made no sense whatsoever, but however different they were, when they were walking off together someplace, not speaking, doing nothing at all, they seemed just the same. In response to it, Dortie began spending more of her time with Russell.

123

They never broke up, but the thing seemed to run its course more or less.. In June, as predicted and expected, Jeremy joined the Army, not making flight school due to a small genetic eye problem, but instead going straight to Fort Benning, Georgia and boot camp. It had been a few months before, when Tonda knew it was perfect and short term that Tonda had done something that later shocked not only Dortie but every teacher at the school. She had applied to college in late May and having first been wait listed, learned of her acceptance to Boston College.

The last night, before Fort Benning, they sat like they had the first night after the party. Shared a cigarette, talked about planes and her mother. When she dropped it on him, the thing about Boston College, he took a long, deep drag off the Camel and exhaling smoke, he smiled at her and said nothing.

* * *

Dortie was a natural mother, enthralled with even the most mundane tasks defining each day. Cleaning soiled, cotton diapers (Pampers were destroying the environment), breast feeding on demand and humming ever so softly to entrance the baby boy to nap. Russell helped with night time and Ivan was a regular presence at the small house, often barreling ass first through the doorway with Loretta slung over his shoulder like a sack of grain.

It seemed that the war in Iraq was getting worse. Each day a boy, some boy from a real family as Ivan always reminded himself, was shot dead by insurgents, blown up by rockets, run through by hidden mortar fire.

‘ People had started honking. Not everyone to be sure, but occasional cars and with some regularity.

On the third day in April, Dortie returned briefly to the line, standing between Russell and her father, with young Cobain bundled in Alpaca fur and stuffed in a baby sling across her front. That day they were joined by a few other protesters with homemade signs of their own. One sign denoted the predictable but effective Lennon quote, "War is Over, Give Peace a Chance." Another said, "Fight Terrorism, Impeach W."

Dortie quickly removed Cobain from the cold, his cameo appearance completed, and went to join her mother to await the return of Ivan and another eagerly awaited stir fry bonanza.

She found Loretta at the window, snow swirling just beyond the pane. Her mother was not slumped over but was staring straight forward, hypnotized by the flakes.

"Little Cobain attended his first peace rally Momma," Dortie proudly proclaimed. "He did real good too, slept right through the whole thing. Daddy called it a non verbal protest," she giggled.

Loretta still stared straight ahead looking beyond the snow and ice field below and when Dortie reached and touched her hand she knew instantly that her mother was dead.

* * *

She was home for Christmas, her senior year at BC, shopping at the local market, adorned in a long black leather coat cut tight on her hips then tapered, when she saw Jeremy again. He was with a blonde woman, dressed conservatively in a green wool sweater with hints of Christmas red on the neck and shoulders.

"Tonda. Tonda Hall. How are you," he said and kissed her cheek.

"Jeremy, my God, it's been what, three years, no four."

"It has," he said, somehow uncomfortable. "Oh," he added, "I'm so sorry, this is my wife Ericka. Ericka, this is my friend from high school Tonda."

"I am a pleasure to be sure," Ericka said, with a thick German accent.

"Ericka's English isn't perfect, she's from Germany. We met through the service."

And really, that was it. An appropriate good bye, a hand shake, some mention of her mother's home cooking and he walked off carrying a bag of groceries and holding Ericka's hand. In her mother's Jeep, Tonda lit a cigarette and thought about BC and the city, missing it all very much. But for a minute she also thought about Dortie.

* * *

They never played the Velvet Underground again at dinner. In fact, Ivan had boxed the old records and put them in a closet. Instead, he would leave the radio on all day as if the voices gave him comfort, as if perhaps Loretta had gone to work for public radio in Canton and would one day communicate with Ivan over the airwaves.

It was the first Friday after Loretta's burial, the first Friday they had not protested in months. Loretta's wheelchair stood folded in the corner and Dortie stood above the wok while Russell tended Cobain. Ivan sat alone at the table, would occasionally smile when Cobain would burp or spit up milk on Russell's shoulder.

It was the radio that did it, pushed Ivan into a terrible mood. The stock market had gone above 10,000, still further proof that the vile conspiracy of big money, oil, war and politics was making the rich American ruling class still richer.

"Turn that bullshit off," Ivan railed.

Dortie started to turn the radio off when another story was introduced.

"And in North Creek, residents are remembering and mourning the loss of twenty five year old Jeremy Dorr, killed yesterday during a missile attack outside of Takrit. Dorr, a seven year veteran of the armed forces, was on a special security detachment with American troops in Iraq…"

Dortie fell forward, catching herself against the radio, her breath lost, her legs and hands shaking.

"Daddy, Daddy, something terrible has happened. It's unbelievably terrible."

＊ ＊ ＊

Tonda recognized Dortie and Ivan in the back of the church almost instantly. Walked discreetly down the aisle and slid in next to her old friend. At first Dortie didn't recognize her, a ganga girl no more, but instead an MBA working just outside of Boston for a commercial loan company, hair drawn perfectly back behind her head in a bun, wearing a long dark coat and gray wool scarf.

Tonda put her hand on Dortie's leg and smiled. Dortie hesitated and then in surprised recognition whispered a bit too loudly, "Tonda Hall, holy shit."

"Dortie," Tonda said in acknowledgment, turning to hug her old friend and acknowledge Ivan with a warm smile and "Hello Mr. Berdosky."

The service had begun without either of them even realizing it and Ivan was almost instantly uncomfortable. "Brass," he hissed under his breath as a Colonel from somewhere spoke warmly, fondly, of Jeremy.

"A trusted leader in the field of battle, respected friend and loving husband and father. In every facet of his life, given for his country, Jeremy Dorr was top notch."

Tonda smiled, remembered the night so many years ago when Jeremy had broken the one game scoring record for the local high school. A record he still held, she suspected. Dortie reached and held Tonda's hand. A flag was presented to a little boy, perhaps four years old, and medal of honor and salute to a blonde woman, the same blonde woman Tonda had met so briefly in the store some years ago, the last time she had seen Jeremy, spoken to him.

Then it was over. Military removed the coffin, bag piper echoing in the early winter air of the church, standing stoically just beyond the intersection where Ivan had begun his many protests.

They walked out of the church together, still holding hands. Leroy Baker was leading the local VFW Honor Guard and a half dozen state troopers stood at attention behind the hearse.

Together they stepped sideways off the church steps, other mourners passing them. They hugged each other, cried intensely, words not coming.

Finally Dortie said, "I have a little boy now."

"You do, my God, how wonderful."

" A little boy, Cobain."

"Cobain, of course Cobain," Tonda smiled.

Dortie lit a cigarette, took a quick drag and as if time had never passed, handed it expertly to Tonda, who took a drag herself. Ivan watched the coffin loaded into the hearse, trying as he might to think about the boy.

He could only think about Loretta, her wheel chair, the wok, old records, their first apartment in Long Island. Ivan turned to Dortie and Tonda and said, "You girls get done here and I'll make you some dinner. How bout it?"

Both girls nodded and smiled as the hearse drove away toward the cemetery, passing the four corners.

TRUE NORTH

The town is always there. It's the place I'm trying to get away from. As far the hell away as I can get. It's the place I've gotta get back to. Feels wrong being away. It's in the middle of things like that. Stuck in my brain in a compartment. One side of the compartment says go. Tired of this shit. Same day, same story. Other side says this is where I might make it. There is a word there. It's "belong." And in the middle of the compartment is the town.

The town is a gutted mill they dress nice for the holidays. White clapboard churches with high steeples built back when we still had Presbyterians. There is a storefront that sold shoes and Pendleton shirts when I was a kid. Now they name sandwiches after ski trails and sell them marked all the hell up to half of New Jersey in ski season. There's a bar named Durant's after the train tycoon that died bankrupt in North Creek. Even he couldn't make it here. There's a broken down building that used to be a wood mill and not far from that a pretty museum where good retired people work hard to find their "belong," after the 401K finally made the suburban commute unnecessary.

I don't have Danny today. He's with his mother. It's near forty degrees at 10:00 p.m. and bad weather ahead, so there's no thought of snow being blown on the mountain for a week anyways. In another compartment in my brain freedom sits right next to boredom and the two are bound together by an unemployment check.

No Durant's for me. Let the high rollers have their Cabernet tonight. I bought a fifth of Jack just before the liquor store closed and stuffed it up under the seat of the GMC. Gas light's been on since Wednesday, but it'll get me home.

Home. There's another compartment. Home is a compartment labeled "all fucked up." That's a compartment we don't visit much. But I'll go up the road now. Mother is tucked in at the home. Already seen her tonight. She asked me why her boy never seems to visit. No recognition.

It needs to get cold quick. Mountain brags about a Thanksgiving opening, but that won't happen. Shoulder season sucks. Cold means money. Cold is good. Cold and warm are in the same compartment.

Up the driveway, the ground still soft. Mud under rear, bald tires. Have to work on that. Save wood tonight anyway. Maybe I could get another couple days in the shop. Not hardly worth the gas money for the ticket I'll get for the uninspected car. I can't buy tires. It's too God damn warm.

Needs to be cold for maybe six straight months. They should make the seasons more certain. Cold November to May and then let the river run and we raft it.

I fill a tumbler full of ice and light a fire anyways. I make a list. Five things I need to get for the main furnace when my ship comes in. My snow ship. The first sip of Jack burns in late death November. I put the tumbler down next to the picture of Danny starting kindergarten. Jackie said she'd save that cute shirt forever, along with the lunch box that was supposed to be a miniature of daddy's work box. Not likely any of that's still around. Find another compartment. No dawdling. By God the Jack was good. I unmuted the TV for weather on the 9s. Cold coming, maybe a week. A picture of a fake turkey strutting oddly below a Canadian front. By God TV is shit.

The stove will need work on the flue. There's a boy in town that can rig it good enough for this year. It still draws good. Then again, maybe I should go south. Warmer climate, maybe some good people. Sometimes I look down at the phone and think I won't be able to dial it someday. That's how it started with my mother. She couldn't dial and couldn't organize even local numbers to call a neighbor. A broken compartment for sure.

Midnight. I'll tell you one thing, I won't go another year like this. Not going to take it sitting down. There was a girl in high school, Kelly Abbott. She went to South Carolina. I could look her up maybe. Probably no good jobs there either. The thing about here for all the other things is that I already got here. In my compartment there and here are the same place.

I step outside before turning in. I carry the Remington to the round stone table. Line up the stock and point the barrel like a compass needle. True North. It's the same gun my father used. Same as always, loaded but the safety on. How do you get to a particular place? Tree limbs crack in the distance like old bones. And then a funny question, who has it better, my mother or father?

Don't stay there. That's what the compass says and don't use. Donnie LaBorne used after doing local time. Took his normal hit but he'd been clean three months. They found him five days later.

Don't dawdle on Danny's mini lunch box neither. No good will come of it. True North is the reminder. Move on.

Yeah, maybe Kelly Abbott. Maybe hear her laugh again like we were at a ball game. The wind picks up slightly. It's barely a whisper but there's something familiar in it. It feels colder.

AFTERWORD

Several notes of thanks are in order.

Debbie Damasevitz and Laurie Lentinello typed early drafts of several of these stories.

Gail Cummings designed the front and back covers using photos taken by Susan Goodspeed. She quickly understood the concept that was being pursued and her creative talents are self evident.

Several members of my family read early drafts of many of these stories and were patient and thoughtful in discussing them. Author Connelly Akstens read The Trick and offered me very encouraging words.

I swear half of writing is confidence. Author Bill McKibben read all nine stories and sent me a long personal note which I read aloud to my wife as she drove south on I-87 to visit our oldest son. His words were so encouraging that I believe they are the reason I was able to round third and finish this project.

And my wife. Yes, she helped extensively with editing, but beyond commas and spelling she was a substantive editor as well. Phrases I remember, "A sixteen year old doesn't talk like that." "The ending, it's not good." "Get it down and then come back and fix it." "Way too awkward." Without her, this remains something I almost finished.